William Henry Linow Barnes

Solid Silver

A Play in Five Acts

William Henry Linow Barnes

Solid Silver
A Play in Five Acts

ISBN/EAN: 9783743389854

Manufactured in Europe, USA, Canada, Australia, Japa

Cover: Foto ©Andreas Hilbeck / pixelio.de

Manufactured and distributed by brebook publishing software
(www.brebook.com)

William Henry Linow Barnes

Solid Silver

A · PLAY

IN FIVE ACTS:

AS PERFORMED AT THE CALIFORNIA THEATRE
SAN FRANCISCO, CAL.

BY

WILLIAM H. L. BARNES.

SAN FRANCISCO:

1871.

SOLID SILVER

A PLAY

IN FIVE ACTS.

AS PERFORMED AT THE CALIFORNIA THEATRE
SAN FRANCISCO, CAL.

BY

WILLIAM H. L. BARNES.

SAN FRANCISCO:

1871.

𝔓ersons of the 𝔇rama,

CALIFORNIA THEATRE,

San Francisco, Cal.

Paul Weir.....................................Mr. JOHN McCULLOUGH

The Earl De la Lande ....Mr. FRED FRANKS

Captain Gerard Morris.....................Mr. W. A. MESTAYER

Mr. Sponge, Senior...........................Mr. HENRY EDWARDS

Mr. Sponge, Junior ....Mr. J. C. WILLIAMSON

Mr. Oldcastle.....................................Mr. SEDLEY SMITH

Mr. Barclay..................................... Mr. GEORGE FRENCH

Leon...Mr. EDMUND LEATHES

Bertha Huntingdon.............................Miss MAY HOWARD

Kate Delaire ....MISS MINNIE WALTON

Lady Emily Peele.........................Miss IMOGENE VANDYKE

Countess De la Lande.........................Miss LOU. JOHNSTON

Mrs. Weir.. .....Mrs. JUDAH

Mrs. Busby ....Mrs. C. R. SAUNDERS

Clementine.. Miss LOU. HARMES

Stage business, cast of characters, relative positions,
etc., arranged and correctly marked by Mr. ROBERT
M. EBERLE, Assistant Stage Manager, California
Theatre.

SOLID SILVER.

ACT FIRST.

SCENE I.—*Room at Huntingdon Towers; half library, half office. Portrait of young lady over door at* L. *Chairs, hat-rack, etc. Large library lamp burning on table at back.*

PAUL.

(*Rising from seat at secretary,* R. II.) I am tired as an old man: I am weary of life and my father's honorable name. I hate this place, and yet can not tear myself away from it. I loathe my daily duties, yet can not abandon them. Those who bring their flatteries here, as slaves bring tribute to a queen, are of no better lineage than I. Yet, poverty leaves me only the solace of honest labor. [*Looking up at the portrait over the mantel,* L. II. 2D E.] Ah! you never change that sweet smile as you seem to listen, while I dare to say—"I love you;" but when your living presence comes and has gone, I deride myself for speaking, even to you, save as a servant speaks. No! my heart shall listen to my reason. If I can not conquer myself, I will at least hug my secret as closely as a murderer holds his, and bewail my dead hope in solitude. I will bury it with labor. [*Sits at desk* R. II. *Enter, unobserved by* PAUL, *Captain* MORRIS, JOHN SPONGE, Sr., and JOHN SPONGE, Jr. R. C.] Yes, by heaven, life is labor. I sentence myself to work as perpetual in degree, if not in kind, as that of the ploughman or railway-navvy. I hail them both as comrades! From this moment I abandon

that unhealthy pride which has so often urged me to seclu-
sion, or to criminal effort to make a gentleman of myself,
such as some of those who haunt her footsteps.

CAPTAIN MORRIS, (R. C.)

(*Interrupting, to* SPONGE, Sr.) Did he speak to me?
Quite eloquent, I declare! Sponge, when you stand for
Parliament, let this orator present your cause to his friends
of the working-classes.

SPONGE, SR. (C.)

Let the man alone. I presume he is Miss Huntingdon's secretary, or steward; isn't he, John?

SPONGE, JR. (L. H.)

Dunno, Governor. Shall I speak to him, Governor?

MORRIS.

As somebody says, be mine the pleasing task. [*Going
up to* PAUL, *who has observed them and then resumed his
work, and tapping him on the shoulder with his cane.*] My
man, you don't know me?

PAUL.

No, sir.

MORRIS.

Where's Miss Huntingdon?

PAUL.

(*Rising.*) I don't know.

MORRIS.

I think you've heard of me! my name is Captain Morris, of the Sixteenth Lancers, cousin to Miss Huntingdon,
and here by her invitation, with my friends, to pass a few
days.

PAUL.

I have heard many things of you, if you are the person
to whom these estates revert in the event of Miss Huntingdon's death, with no children surviving her.

MORRIS.

That 's me. So far as I know, the likeness is correct, Sponge, eh ?

SPONGE, SR.

[*Sponge, Jr. retires up, examining books, pictures, etc.*] He knows you well enough for the present. Don't push the man's knowledge too far ; it won't pay.

MORRIS.

Since you do recall me, my man, allow me to ask if you are too far removed from the position of butler to tell me what apartments have been reserved for my friends and myself?

PAUL.

I will ring for a servant, who can inform you, sir.
                         [*Rings bell.*
      Enter LEON, (R. 1 E.)

Leon, these gentlemen say they are expected guests. Ask Mrs. Busby where their apartments are and show them the way.

LEON.

Madame Busby has already informed me where they repose themselves. Messieurs, I am at your service.
                [*Crosses up to* L. 3 E.

SPONGE, JR. (L. II., *back to audience.*)

Go easy a minute, Frenchy ; I'm looking round a trifle. I say, Mr. ——

PAUL. (R. II.)

Weir.

SPONGE, JR.

Weir, then, who 's that handsome gal·hanging over the mantel there ? [*All turn towards* L. II. *and look at picture.*]

PAUL.

That is a portrait of Miss Huntingdon, the owner of this house.

SPONGE, SR. (C.)

What? let me see it! God, how healthy she looks! [*To* MORRIS.] Say, I thought you told me ——

MORRIS. (R. C.)

Well, well, never mind now, Sponge; let us go to our apartments. [*To* LEON.] Confound you, sir, why don't you go? What are you waiting for, you idiot?

LEON.

I don't know, Monsieur. Messieurs, the father and son will repose in those apartments, [*pointing to door* L. 3 E. *of scene,*] and will use this one at their convenience. I will show this gentleman his apartment in another part of the house. [*Cross to* R. H. 3 E. LEON *and* MORRIS *exit* R. 3 E.; SPONGE, Jr. *and* SPONGE, Sr. L. 3 E. *In a moment,* SPONGE, Sr. *returns.* PAUL *seats himself at desk.*]

SPONGE, SR.

Excuse me, young gentleman, no offense I hope, in asking a question or two? no questions—no lies, is the old saying; no questions—no knowledge, is my motto. You see, I'm in a sort of financial bother which I don't like, and I don't mind paying, if that will help me out of it. Is that really Miss Huntingdon's picture up there?

PAUL.

I told you before that it was, did I not?

SPONGE, SR.

So you did. But a man must be told a thing twice, and oftener, which he does n't want to believe, before he takes it all in, don't you see? Painted some time ago, you said?

PAUL.

It was taken in the spring. You won't see many faces as radiant with the grace and beauty of youth and perfect health as hers. Angels in heaven may look more pure, but there are none more angelic than she. Why ——

SPONGE, SR.

Yes, yes; I understand all that, and am glad she's

good, for the comfort of her friends when she's gone. I'm going to get in some of it myself one of these days. No time just now. How long can she live, now, do you think?

PAUL.

I hope many, many years will pass before nature will claim its debt of her sweet life.

SPONGE, SR.

You hope so? Well, christianly speaking, so do I; but in a business point of view, I can't admit the proposition. I supposed now she was feeble, decrepit, consumptive, and couldn't hang on, say, well—not much beyond the close of the present fiscal year.

PAUL.—(*starting up.*)

Who told you such a falsehood as that? Feeble? Decrepit? I wish you could have seen her this morning, coming up the avenue on her huge thoroughbred horse "Titan." He was swinging along, with eyes of fire and wide-opened nostrils; his great brown limbs striking now on the turf and now on the gravel, his slender mane standing straight out, like a flag in a hurricane—just as he came in winner at the Ascot last year; while she rode him so gloriously and fearlessly, with such a color in her cheeks and such a light in her eyes, that no living man could associate the idea of decay and death with her, and none but a double-dyed scoundrel could wish her dead. Who told you that lie, I say?

SPONGE, SR.

Softly, softly, my young friend; I don't like your language, and your manner is unbusiness-like in the extreme. I wish to regard the subject without nonsensical enthusiasm. I'm too old for it, by Jove! I only said what I supposed to be a fact, and wanted you to make me more certain of; and I've got your views as fully as I want 'em, too.

PAUL.

Excuse me if I am rude to you, an old man and a stranger; but I could not endure to hear Miss Huntingdon so spoken of.

B

SPONGE, SR.

You are a relative, I presume ?

PAUL.

I am simply her agent, secretary and servant. My father was vicar of this parish, and greatly beloved by her's. So on his death, and for my mother's sake, I was appointed to my present place, and have held it five years.

SPONGE, SR.

[*All through the following dialogue* SPONGE Sr. *tries to meddle with the papers and books in the desk.* PAUL *prevents him.*]

Keep the accounts, know how the money tide rises and falls, rentes, consols, three per cents., and all that, I suppose ?

PAUL.

Oh, yes! I keep the accounts, and something beside!

SPONGE, SR.

What's that ?

PAUL.

My own counsel. [SPONGE *tries to examine ledger.* PAUL *closes it and lays his hand on it.*]

SPONGE, SR.

Hum. I suppose, now, there are no incumbrances upon the estate ?

PAUL.

None.

SPONGE, SR.

No timber being cut either, I should say ? [*Trying to examine papers in pigeon-holes of desk.*]

PAUL.

None. [*Closes desk, locks it, and stands with his back leaning against it.*]

SPONGE, SR.

Any likelihood of marriage ?

PAUL.

I do not know.

SPONGE, SR.

You ought to know. Your opportunities for observation are A 1, gilt-edged, as we say of paper. If you don't know, I do.

PAUL—(*starts from desk.*)

What do you know? How *can* you, who are a stranger to the family, know anything on such a subject? She has no lover, at least, no declared lover; certainly none who would dare approach her.

SPONGE, SR.

For all that she will marry soon, and I lay you something handsome I can name the man.

PAUL.

Who, who is he? (*Advances* c.)

SPONGE, SR.

Captain Gerard Morris, reversioner of her estates and her maternal cousin. He is a fascinating dog, detested by men, I admit, but adored by women, and she can't withstand him. As for him, ecod, he must marry her or——

PAUL.

Or what?

SPONGE, SR.

Never you mind! That's my business, and John Sponge, sr., proposes to attend to it. That's what he's here for, and—— [*Takes Stage* L. II.]

Enter LEON, (c. *from* R.)

[*Bringing hat boxes, portmanteaus, etc., which he places on the floor near the door* L. 3 E.]

LEON—(*advances* c.)

Monsieur Paul, I know not what I shall do. The big one swear at his apartment and demand the best brandy already four times, and the little one smoke his nasty pipe in his room, and so Madame Busby is lunatic with the annoyance of it.

PAUL.

Mr. Sponge, you had better remind your son that this is not an inn. As to the other, Leon, he must go his own way. Let him alone, and quiet Mrs. Busby as best you can.

LEON. (c.)

She shall not be quiet while she will inhale the odor of that pipe. [LEON *retires up stage.*]

SPONGE, SR. (*advancing towards* WEIR.)

Good night, Mr. Weir. Thanks for favors. I'll make that pipe sing in shortmetre. D—n that boy! he's as vicious as a monkey, and has no more manners than a Bow-street bailiff. As for the other, Mrs. Busby had better adapt her temper to his. He's a born devil, if ever there was one, and must stay here as master, either by marriage or death. To me, as a business proposition, it don't matter which. But she'd find it easier to die and yield the lands, than live and share them with him. But business is business. Good night, good night.

[*Exit* L. 3 E.

LEON.

Where's Mrs. Busby, Leon? [LEON *advances*, L. C.] I hope you left her more at ease than you said.

PAUL.

By no means. When I last saw her in the corridor, she was all ready to make a descent on the smoker at least, if not the drunkard, as she called them. I think I hear her now, sir. [*Looking off* R. 1 E.]

PAUL.

Heaven forbid; I will go myself and dissuade her from the attack.

LEON.

I will follow sir, but at a safe distance (R. 1 E.)

[*Exeunt.*

[*Enter young* SPONGE, L. 3 E. *When* SPONGE, *Jr. enters, he picks up portmanteau near door, brings it forward; sits in arm-chair* R. *of* L. *table; takes key out of pocket, unlocks portmanteau, and commences to take out things; shirts, collars, suspenders, slippers, bootjack, etc.; is smoking a big pipe, and making lots of smoke with it.*]

SPONGE, JR.

This is comfortable, indeed, and a mighty fine house ;
beats all I ever was allowed to put my feet inside of.
How such an up-and-down vagabond as our captain could
come of such stock I don't understand. The governor
and I aren't gentlemen, and don't pretend to be. We're
business men, and our connection with the blooded ones
only helps them to get to the devil a trifle faster than
they otherwise would. But this one — he does, every day
of his life, what we could not do, and never blushes at
anything but his brandy when it goes the wrong way.
[Mrs. BUSBY *enters*, R. 1 E., *walks up to* SPONGE ; *stands gaz-
ing at him in amazement.*]   If it wasn't too dear a luxury,
I'd wish him dead and pay for his funeral, I would, by—
[*perceives* Mrs. BUSBY] Hullo ! my charmer, happy to see
you ; sit down while I hunt up my bootjack and get these
French boots off my trotters. Then — [*gets down on his
knees at portmanteau.*]

MRS. BUSBY.

Sir, Mister, whatever you are, I came to say ——

SPONGE, JR. (*looking up.*)

No apologies, Ma'am, I beg [*puff*]. You needn't excuse
yourself to me for crowing in your own barnyard. In
your place I'll do the same, [*puff*] and you're safe here,
I'll swear ; [*puff*] your face would protect you among
the Mormons [*puff*]. But don't you look in my mirror
with that cap on. It would shiver to a thousand atoms,
[*puff*] and I hain't seen such a costume as that since my
grandma used to put me in my little bed. Ah, here's the
bootjacker ! so now I'll have these calfskins off in a
moment.

MRS. BUSBY.

If it's for calfskin, you'd better pull your hide off—
the whole of it ! Of all the impudent young dogs, to talk
that way to a decent old body like me ! Young man,
what do you take me for ?
[*All through the dialogue, and until he puts pipe out, he
puffs the smoke in Mrs. B.'s face, and she keeps coughing
and shows her annoyance.*]

SPONGE, JR.

Don't want you ; won't take you on any terms. How old are you ? Where'd you get that awning over your front door ? Where's your dagger, Lady Macbeth ? Blessed if you don't look homicidal, anyhow ! Come near me, and I'll brain you with my bootjack, and kiss you afterwards. [*Stands in attitude with bootjack.*]

MRS. BUSBY.

You insolent little villain, look at me. I'm a respectable woman, and have been housekeeper in Huntingdon Towers [*coughs*] ever since its present mistress was born, [*coughs*] and I'll have you to understand that no such creature as you ever got between sheets in this house before [*coughs*]. I came to ask you to put up that rascally pipe, or go down to the smoking room and blow your little brains out with tobacco there [*coughs*]. It fills the house with the odor of a tavern, and poisons every breath of air in it.

SPONGE, JR.

Now you speak of it, Mrs. Johnson, I think I smell something myself.

MRS. BUSBY.

Faugh ! Will you put that pipe out or not ? And don't you dare to call me Mrs. Johnson again, Mr. what's your name.

SPONGE, JR.

To oblige you, Grandma, [*Mrs. B. appears very indignant*], I will quench it. There she goes. [*Puts pipe down.*] My name is not what's y'r name any more than your own. It is John Sponge, Jr. My Governor's somewhere about, pumping the clerk, or whatever he is, whom we saw when we came in.

MRS. BUSBY.

I'd like to know how you got in !

SPONGE, JR.

Well, I won't mind telling you, as it is you, dearest. Captain Morris invited us here to see his estates, on which

we have made large advances to put him straight at
Tattersall's—for he lost heavy at the last Derby, I tell you.
Now you know me and why I'm here—anything more,
Mrs. Dobson?

MRS. BUSBY.

No, sir. I knew all you have told me before you said
it. Only let me give you my opinion that Captain Morris'
chances to get these estates, as you call them, ain't worth
a dairy full of milk in a thunder shower.

SPONGE, JR.

Indeed!

MRS. BUSBY.

No, sir, and you won't think so either when you see the
present holder ; and if her giving out is the only way for
you to get your money back, why, let it go, and do you
start for town by the morning train, and pick up a new
pigeon for plucking.

SPONGE, JR.

I wish you'd put all that in writing and hand it to me
in the morning. [*Gapes.*] It's a jolly opinion! Ain't
you sorry for us?

MRS. BUSBY.

No, sir ; serves you right. [*Takes stage* R. H.] You
asked my opinion. Now you've got it, I hope you like it.

Enter SPONGE, SR.

[*Advances* C, *with carpet bag, which he picks up near door,
where* LEON *has placed it.*]

SPONGE, JR.

Hullo, Governor. Glad you've come ; was afraid one
time I was going to be sacrificed. But it's all right now.
The ancient and me are at peace. My pipe is out, but
she holds fire still. [*Gets up ; puts valise* L. H.]

SPONGE, SR., (C.)

Hold your tongue. Excuse me, ma'am, can I do anything for you? If not, I'll go about my business, which
is to prepare myself for bed. [*Pulls out a nightcap and
puts it on, and takes off his coat.* Mrs. BUSBY *precipitately*

retires R. 1 E.] Thank God she's gone. John, if I see that pipe in your mouth again while we're here, dam'me, I'll jam it down your throat, bowl and all. We've got trouble enough without a war with women. Do you know where the captain's room is? If you do, go there. If you don't, find it, and tell him I want to see him here, at once.

SPONGE, JR., (L. II.)

All right, Governor, just as you say, but I don't believe he'll come. [*Crosses* R. II. *in front.*]

SPONGE, SR., (*savagely*).

Why not?

SPONGE, JR.

You know yourself he's likely to be very obstinate at this hour.

SPONGE, SR., (*sits* R. *of* L. *table.*)

Tell him he must come, and while you're gone I'll open my writing case and get out the documents. [*Exit* SPONGE, Jr., R. 3 E.] These are my persuaders. Bow-street and the debtors' lock-up are powerful arguments. Let me see—four and two are six, which I took of him myself; three and one is four, I bought of the Levi's, accepted by his uncle, Colonel Delaire—only the acceptances are mistakes of my captain, which would land him in Newgate or Botany Bay, or wherever else they send blunderers in chirography. The game is almost played out.

[*Enter* Captain MORRIS, *in dressing gown, slippers, etc., accompanied by* SPONGE, Jr.]

MORRIS.

My dear Sponge, why send this cub of yours for me at this time? [*Lounges in chair near desk*, R. II.]

SPONGE, SR.

Because I wanted you.

MORRIS.

There is nothing come due since we parted that I remember, and by Jove, I've signed away my soul to you already.

SPONGE, SR.

Not to me ; to the devil, you mean.

MORRIS.

It's all one, Sponge ; but what's up?

SPONGE, SR.

I want a talk with you. The matter is just here : I lend you £10,000 on your own notes, and take up £5,000 of acceptances of Colonel Delaire, your uncle, which you had discounted with the Levis.

MORRIS.

Is that all? Do you know I was afraid it was 20,000 ? I have been more moderate than I thought.

SPONGE, SR.

Never fear, it will be larger than it is! Well, for this £15,000 you give me as security a mortgage on your reversionary interest in the Huntingdon estates.

MORRIS.

Good security, isn't it?   .

SPONGE, SR.

In one sense, yes. But to persuade me to take it, you tell me the present holder is in feeble health and likely to drop off any time, while from all I see and hear, she is likely to outlive you, and me too! Morris, I always believed you to be a villain, and now I'd swear to it.

MORRIS.

Your statement presents all the phenomena of virtuous truth, Sponge. What next? I reserve comment.

SPONGE, SR.

Ah, you reserve your defense, as gentlemen of your sort say before the magistrates. Well, reserve it for the night ; I'll go to town to-morrow and have you brought to book, as sure as my credit is good on 'Change for what I put my name to.

MORRIS.

As you like, Sponge. I'm so nearly at bay that it

c

makes small odds to me what you do ; but it strikes me, you had best allow me to play my last card, which is a tolerable good one, for our mutual benefit, and it may win for us both.

SPONGE, JR.

But, Morris, you've such a deuced bad name in this house ; worse here, I should say, than in London. They paint the lily, by Jove, even here.

MORRIS, (*indifferently.*)

How do you know ?

SPONGE, JR.

I heard the old woman, who called on me so politely a while ago, and that French waiter, discussing you as I came along the corridor. It's no matter what they said in detail ; the total was a bad balance to your moral credit.

MORRIS.

Don't be so sure, my infant Shylock. But as I was saying, [*to* SPONGE, Sr.] I think the best way is not to abandon yourself to despair till I have lost all ; and all is not yet lost, by a long shot.

SPONGE, SR.

You mean that marriage is the game you will play?

MORRIS.

Exactly so. It is the only alternative from the death I promised you, and —— [*rising, going up* C.]

SPONGE, SR.

Well ? Well ?

MORRIS.

You shall have one or the other within the month. Good night. [*Exit* Captain MORRIS, R. 3 E.

SPONGE, JR.

Governor, that's a very bad lot. [*Rising from sofa and coming to* L. *of table.*]

SPONGE, SR.

So it is. Where's my prayer book ? [*After a pause,* SPONGE, Jr. *and* SPONGE, Sr. *exchange looks.* SPONGE, Sr.

opens carpet-bag, takes out prayer book.] What are the psalms for to-day? What day is this? To-morrow, Bulger's note is due, and we've got insurance coming in on that loss of the " Comet." Yes, to-day's the twenty-fifth, and I'll read those for to-day, to please your mother.

SPONGE, JR.

It's a big loss, but I'll stand my share of it, and drop the whole job, if you will consent. There's something in such a conspiracy against an orphan girl's life or property that tastes worse than bad tobacco and stale beer to me.

SPONGE, SR.

Don't be a fool, and don't interrupt your father's evening devotions. Business is business, and we'll do no more till to-morrow. [*Reads very busily.*]

SPONGE, JR.

Certainly, Governor! By the way, did I tell you I heard great news of the Cornwall shares, just as we were leaving town? Snapper met me on 'Change, and says he ——

SPONGE, SR.

(*Throwing down the book on table and rising very nimbly.* SPONGE, Jr. *rises same time and follows his father toward* c.) No, you did *not*. What was it? If they advance five per cent., will sell all ours, and give 'em five hundred more seller thirty. We'll sell on a rising market, and leave fools to unload in the panic. How much advance, eh? [SPONGE, Sr. *speaks rapidly and in a very excited manner.*]

[SPONGE, Jr. *takes up the book, seats himself in his father's chair very deliberately, and reads with great affected diligence.*]

SPONGE, SR.

Come, John! Don't keep me waiting all night, John!

SPONGE, JR.

I ain't a fool. Don't interrupt your son's evening devotions to the golden calf. Business is business, and we will do no more till to-morrow.

CURTAIN.

ACT SECOND.

SCENE I.—*Drawing-room at Huntingdon Towers, elegantly furnished.* KATE DELAIRE *discovered sitting at table at* R. *arranging flowers; near her stands* CLEMENTINE, BERTHA'S *maid.*

KATE.

Clementine, where's your mistress?

CLEMENTINE.

She is out on horseback, Miss Kate.

KATE.

Did she go alone?

CLEMENTINE.

The Captain accompanied her, Miss Kate.

KATE.

How she endures him I can't understand; interfering, as he does, with every act of her life, and as full of dictation as a full-grown husband. Yet she only says, "Yes, Captain Morris," and "No, cousin," instead of cuffing his big ears and sending him, like one of his own soldiers, to the right-about. Bah! it makes me sick, I declare!

CLEMENTINE.

For all that, he is by no means sure of his ground. He offered me a guinea, the day before yesterday, to ask her what she thought of him, and report her answer.

KATE.

No! Did he, though? It would not cost him a guinea to get my opinion of him.

CLEMENTINE.

Don't you think him handsome, at least?

KATE.

He's a perfect ogre! But handsome or homely, I would not have such a lover if I lived unmarried in this life, and hereafter nursed cats in the lower region, as they say old maids do.

CLEMENTINE.

I think all men would make slaves of all women, if they had the courage.

KATE. ·

Well, my husband may bully me, and I presume he will—the brutes generally do ; but my lover *shan't*, that's certain. Did you take his guinea, Clementine?

CLEMENTINE.

I don't look a woman to refuse a guinea, do I? Of course I took it, and also the brandyfied kiss he graciously bestowed along with it, without a murmur.

KATE.

Did he have the impudence to do that? And you allowed it? Clementine, you ought to be ashamed.

CLEMENTINE.

Bless you, Miss Kate, servants get used to that, when men like the Captain are in the way.

KATE.

Clementine, I'll tell Miss Bertha, as soon as I see her. I will, indeed.

CLEMENTINE.

Oh, I told her myself.

KATE.

What did she say?

CLEMENTINE.

She laughed, and said she wouldn't be in my place for a good deal. Ah! I hear her coming in the hall door. Excuse me, Miss Kate. [*Courtsies and goes towards door at back and centre of scene.*]

Enter BERTHA, *in riding habit, tall hat wrapped with white veil, riding whip, etc.*

BERTHA.

(*Kissing Kate, throws herself into sofa,* L. II.) Good morning, Kate. Oh! I am so hot! I've had such a race on dear old "Titan," and we've both come in piping, I can tell you. Oh, Kate! where did you get those lovely flowers? I went all through the garden, yesterday, and found none worth picking; they were all wilted and dusty, as if they were tired of life, as, heigho! I am, sometimes, myself.

KATE.

The gardener brought me these splendid roses; put some in your hair when you change your dress. Here's two beauties! [BERTHA *takes roses and puts them in her dress.*] But this heliotrope I got from Mr. Weir.

BERTHA.

Let's see it. That reminds me, Clementine; tell Mr. Weir I wish to see him. [*Exit* CLEMENTINE R. 3 E. BERTHA *takes the heliotrope, and, as she talks, removes the roses from her habit, lets them fall on the floor, and replaces them with the heliotrope.*] I have'nt told you what I've done this morning. First and foremost, I ran away from Captain Morris. That's the third time this week. Ha! ha! ha! His pretty hack may do for Hyde Park, but he can't keep the pace with "Titan!" You see, we rode quietly enough down the avenue as far as the big oaks, and then I turned off and rode Titan straight at the high hedge that shuts in the deer park. He flew it like a bird, and as I rode off, I heard the captain ask the groom, in the ugliest tone, where the —— (such a naughty awful word, Katie,) the gate was? I'm afraid the captain is unprepared to have his neck broken, [*enter* MORRIS, *unperceived, in riding costume,*] and I'm afraid he's a trifle timid. It's a hard thing to say of a soldier and my own cousin; but if he don't fight for his country any more desperately than he rides for me, he won't be found among the dead or the wounded.

KATE.

Don't waste any more precious breath on him. Let us
drop him where you did. What next?

BERTHA.

Then I went past dear old Mrs. Weir's, and there I met
the De Landes and Lady Emily Peele on their way to
see the preparations for my birthday fête, and then gal-
loped home. That's my morning's work ; what do you
think of it?

MORRIS, (*coming forward* c.)

If you appeal to me, Bertha, I can only say I hope the
pleasure you seem to have given others is equal to my
annoyance, though I ought to be resigned to such treat-
ment when I see you so delighted to retail it.

BERTHA.

Cousin, I'm sorry I annoyed you, and regret you over-
heard what I said to Kate just now. Please forgive me !
[*Gives her hand to* MORRIS.]

KATE, (*aside.*)

Just hear her beg that man's pardon ! I'll try my hand.
[KATE *rises, and advances to* MORRIS.] Captain Morris, I
regret my pleasure disturbed your equanimity, but I never
enjoyed anything more in my life. Ha ! Ha ! It's the
only real happiness you have given me since you came
to the Towers, and it will do, sir, if I have no more
till——

MORRIS.

Well, till when ?

KATE.

Till you go away. [BERTHA *retires up stage, looking at
the flowers, etc.*]

MORRIS.

I'd like to be equally frank. I'd love to tell you, my
dear cousin, what I think of your interesting self.

KATE.

Give your opinion, Gerard, to those who seek it. One
thing you may be sure of——

MORRIS.

What is that, pray ?

KATE.

I wouldn't give a guinea for it.   I might give a kiss ;
it is easily minted, but a guinea—never!   Ha! Ha!
Ha!

MORRIS, (*aside.*)

What can she mean ?   Can Clementine have betrayed
my confidence ?   [*To* KATE.] I don't understand you, but
I don't know it's worth while making the attempt.

KATE.

I'd advise you not to try.   I don't think you'd hear
anything to your advantage.

BERTHA, (*comes down* C.)

Come, dear friends, a truce to quarreling.   [KATE *and*
MORRIS *separate annoyed.*]   This lovely morning breathes
nothing but peace and good will out of doors.   Let us
have sunshine indoors as well.   Excuse my preaching,
Kate, darling ; but I am growing old, and can take liberties
with young people.   Only think !   I shall be twenty-one
to-morrow.

KATE.

I shall be earliest to bid you good morning, dear !   first
to wish the close of the year may [*looking at* MORRIS,] see
you still heart whole and fancy free, excepting always
myself and Titan.

MORRIS.

No one will desire your happiness more than I, Bertha,
or do more to contribute towards it than ——

Enter LEON, (L. 3 E.)

LEON.

The Earl and Countess De la Lande, Lady Emily Peele,
and Mr. Barclay have arrived, Miss Huntingdon.

MORRIS.

Show them up, sir.

LEON.

I beg pardon, Miss Huntingdon.   [*Advances a little.*]
D

MORRIS.

Don't you hear me, you French fool ; show them up.

LEON.

I beg pardon, Mademoiselle.

BERTHA.

Do as Captain Morris says, Leon.

LEON.

Certainly, Mademoiselle.   [*Exit* LEON, L. 3 E.

KATE, (*aside.*)

That Leon is a darling. If I had a guinea, I'd give it him, and I could almost give him a kiss, *a la* Morris.

[*Enter* Earl *and* Countess DE LA LANDE, Lady EMILY PEELE, *and* Mr. BARCLAY. *All exchange greetings.* Countess *kisses* BERTHA. BERTHA *asks them to sit.* MORRIS *sits in arm-chair,* L. *corner.* Countess *and* EMILY *on sofa.* BARCLAY *takes chair back of sofa, and sits between sofa and* MORRIS. Earl *takes chair from near stand,* L. C., *brings it forward and sits.* BERTHA *takes chair from back of table.*]

COUNTESS.

[*To* BERTHA.] Well, dear, we've reached here almost as soon as you ; though you went flying across country ! [*To* Captain MORRIS.] Why, Captain, you're in riding costume ! Were you with Bertha ? We did not see you, did we, Emily ?

LADY EMILY.

No, unless he was the young gentleman, with his hands full of heliotrope, whom I saw her salute so graciously in the avenue, as she charged along before us.

KATE.

So, indeed ? I think she has the flowers now, in return for the salute. Oh ! Bertha, you hypocrite !

BERTHA.

Hush, Kate, I beg you !

MORRIS.

No, Lady Emily, I was not the individual with the flowers; he was probably the gardener, or some such fellow.

KATE.

Oh, no! Captain Morris hasn't been gathering flowers. He has been riding—I should say *hunting*.

BARCLAY.

Hunting? This is not the season; won't be for four months to come.

KATE.

For all that, he *was* hunting. Weren't you, Gerard?

MORRIS.

I was *not*.

KATE.

Yes, he was, though — hunting *gates* in hedges over which Bertha *leaped*. Could not find any! Ha! ha! Out of season, I think he said, and so rode home, like a good boy. Ha! ha!

MORRIS, (*aside.*)

D—n her!

BERTHA.

Kate, if you don't control that mischievous tongue of yours, you shan't stay in the room. I'll send you out of doors, as they do naughty children.

KATE (*mischievously*).

Shall I get you some more heliotrope, dear, when I go? Perhaps you'll go for that, yourself.

BERTHA, (*pettishly.*)

Kate, you're a nuisance. [*Rises.*]

EARL.

Miss Bertha, I would like to look at your efforts in decorations for the birthday *fête*. I hear they are extremely tasteful.

BERTHA.

I think they are pretty; but don't give me credit for them.

COUNTESS.

Who is entitled to it, then, if you are not ?

BERTHA.

Mr. Weir, the manager of the estates since papa died.
He has made these plans, and, in fact, designed everything for me ; and here he is. [*Enter* PAUL WEIR, (R. 3 E.)
with roll of drawings under his arm.] Allow me to
present Mr. Weir. [PAUL *advances* R. H. ; *bows civilly ;
no one returns his bow, but all simply stare at him, and then
turn away.* KATE, *annoyed at the manner in which they
treat* PAUL, *bows very politely to him, and looks indignant at
the others.*] Mr. Weir, excuse me ; when I sent for you,
I was alone ; at least, only Miss Delaire was here. I
wished to enquire if you had completed the design for
covering the pavilion ?

PAUL.

It is finished. I have brought it with me. [*Hands it
to her, and retires* R. H.]

BERTHA.

[*Crosses* L. C. *with drawing. They crowd round her.*]
Oh ! is not this lovely ? Just look, all of you ! [*All
gather and examine.*]

LADY EMILY, (L. C.)

[*To* BARCLAY.] Is not that the man with the heliotrope
whom we passed in the park ?
[Countess *and* Earl, *after glancing at drawing, retire
up.*]

BARCLAY (L. H.)

I don't know ; perhaps he is ; but these working men
all look alike. What is he, captain ? Belongs to the
place, I suppose ?

MORRIS, (L.)

You'd think this place belonged to him, by the way he
is allowed to direct its affairs. The same fuss is made
always that you see now made over these very common
designs of his. [MORRIS *moves towards* C. EMILY, BAR-
CLAY *retire up a little, and converse with* Earl, Countess.]

KATE, *(advancing towards* MORRIS.)

Oh, yes, very common ; but ladies, [*all turn towards* MORRIS,] you should see the *captain's designs.* He has some that take in the *whole estate.* Have'nt you, captain ? He's too modest to exhibit them in public, but we'll all hear of them in good time. Ha ! ha !

MORRIS.

I have nothing of the sort. [*Takes* PAUL'S *designs from* BERTHA'S *hands, rolls them up and throws them contemptuously on the floor towards* PAUL. PAUL *picks them up and holds them.*]

KATE.

You know you have, but *n'importe!* they won't be adopted. [*Goes up* C.]

COUNTESS.

Come ! let us go to the pavilion, and Bertha, dear, please order us something to eat, for I'm nearly famished. [Countess *takes* BARCLAY'S *arm;* Lady EMILY *and the* Earl *move towards door,* R. U. E.]

MORRIS, (*crosses to* R. C.)

[*To* PAUL.] Here, you! Have some refreshment prepared in the dining-room when we return !

KATE, (*advancing* L. C.)

And after that, please, Mr. Weir, tell Clementine that Captain Morris wishes to speak with her privately, on business of importance, at her earliest convenience !

BERTHA.

Kate, I wish you'd hush.
[*All commence to leave the room; the* Earl *takes* Lady EMILY *and* KATE.]

MORRIS.

[*Advancing to* BERTHA.] Console me by accepting my escort. [*Offers his arm and stands waiting with it extended.*]

BERTHA.

[*To* MORRIS.] Certainly. [BERTHA *advances to* PAUL.] I will relieve you of the annoyance of accompanying us. [*Exeunt all but* MORRIS, PAUL *and* BERTHA ; *she takes the* .

drawings from PAUL'S *hands; he stands with eyes fixed on the carpet.*] I know you will do me the justice to believe I did not intend to expose you to this great rudeness. If you only knew ——

MORRIS.

We are waiting, Miss Huntingdon.

[BERTHA *takes the Captain's arm and starts to go with him, falters and looks back at* PAUL. MORRIS *takes* BERTHA *off* R. 3 E. *and appears very much annoyed.* PAUL *crosses to* L. H. *in front, watching them.*]

PAUL.

I am no man if I remain here longer. This ceaseless hunger of my heart : this suffocating tide of hopeless love, these bitter jealousies and vain regrets, will drive me mad. She reads my heart. I saw just now the light of pity shining from her eyes, as speechless stars shine from the vault of night, far, far above me. I can endure no more without the loss of that proud self-respect which has so long restrained my traitor tongue. Why should I suffer thus ? I owe no duty which should hold me in slavery to a wretch like him. Yes, I will go ; but until then, let him beware. Let him win her, if he can ; squander her fortune, and break her innocent heart at last. I can not interpose to save her. But let him beware, I say, once more to lord it over me, or turn again towards me his cool, contemptuous glance. He'll find more manhood in me than his Lordship bargains for.   [*Exit* R. 1 E.

SCENE II.—*Corridor in Huntingdon Towers. High-paneled wainscoting and windows with diamond-shaped panes of glass.*

Enter Mrs. BUSBY, (R. 1 E.)

I believe I'm going crazy ! To see these men doing the Lord knows what, and plotting to kidnap Lord knows who under our very noses, is enough to worrit one's seven senses to nothing ! I wish I were a man ! But oh, Lord ! what's the good of wishing ? and I'm delaying *here* chattering away to myself, when I should be about my business, and there's enough of it, I should say. [*Crosses and meets* SPONGE, *Jr. entering* L. 1 E.]

SPONGE, JR.

Good morning, Mrs. Busby. You look as fresh as a daisy. You're a happy woman to-day, to judge by your smiling face.

MRS. BUSBY, (*simpering.*)

I don't know about my looks, Mr. Sponge. I'm as the Lord made me. But I'm not smiling, nor yet happy.

SPONGE, JR.

Nothing is the matter with you, Buzzy, I hope.

MRS. BUSBY.

You hope! much you can hope in this world or the next, with your schemes to destroy everybody's peace; and don't you call me "Buzzy." I'm not buzzy.

SPONGE, JR.

Count me out in that game, my blossom! I've not been here a week for nothing.

MRS. BUSBY.

Your father and the Captain are in it, though, and that's the same thing.

SPONGE, JR.

Don't visit those venerable sinners' crimes on this generation! I say nothing for the Captain, he's a bad lot, and always was. But the Governor can't hurt! He'd be a nice old ambassador at the court of Cupid. I don't believe you'd listen to him.

MRS. BUSBY.

Me listen to him? I wish you would both go home—that's my heart's desire morning, noon and night!

SPONGE, JR.

Well, he won't and I can't.

MRS. BUSBY.

Why not? *you* don't expect to marry an heiress and settle here?

SPONGE, JR.

I don't want an heiress ; I am one myself. I want a wife, and I'd as soon settle for her here as anywhere.

MRS. BUSBY.

And *you're* in love ?   Oh, Lord !

SPONGE, JR.

Buzzy, I'm a goner! dead in love, and hopeless besides.

MRS. BUSBY.

Clementine, I presume.

SPONGE, JR.

Clementine ·be— blessed ! Don't make fun of me, but it's Miss Kate.

MRS. BUSBY.

Go home and get cured. It's no use. *I* know her.

SPONGE, JR.

Don't you think I stand to win at any odds ?

MRS. BUSBY.

Honestly, now ?

SPONGE, JR.

Honor bright and shining.

MRS. BUSBY.

Oh ! ask herself. Say some of the polite things you've said to me ; you'll get your answer.

SPONGE, JR.

I dare n't ! but Buzzy, dear, I'd make a gilt-edged husband for her.   She's poor and I'm rich now, and when the Governor is translated I'll just be rotten with money. I'd give it all for one smile, this minute. It isn't more than two to one against me ?

MRS. BUSBY.

I think they'd all be against you. I want to spare your feelings, young man, for you've been always *so* considerate of mine, and therefore would simply remark that I am afraid she would not touch you with a pair of tongs !

SPONGE, JR.

I don't think, myself, I'd let her handle me with that sort of hardware. Thank you for putting it so mildly ; but——

MRS. BUSBY.

You know you are not fit for her, if you know anything.

SPONGE, JR.

I'm old enough.

MRS. BUSBY.

Old in sin, I'll warrant.

SPONGE, JR.

That's true, Buzzy, God knows. I've wished a thousand times, since I saw her, that I could wash the stains of London life out of my soul, and be as pure as she is.

MRS. BUSBY.

It can't be done. [*Sighing.*]

SPONGE, JR.

It can't! My heart's all right, my head is level, and I've lots of resolution. You'll see. I'm bound to win. I'm getting courage every hour. Oh! here she comes. I don't know how it is ; when I think of her, I'm as bold as a lion, and when I see her, I feel as weak as water !

Enter KATE, *with small basket,* L. 1 E. *She crosses to* Mrs. B. ; *then looks over her shoulder at* SPONGE, Jr. *who stands bowing timidly.*]

SPONGE, JR.

Good morning.

KATE—(*bows slightly.*)

Good morning.

SPONGE, JR.

Nice morning.

KATE.

Yes.

SPONGE, JR.

Are you pretty well ? You look very pretty — well. Yes, it's a nice morning.

E

KATE—(*turns away.*)

Oh! Mrs. Busby, I am so glad to find you. You're dreadfully wanted in the pavilion — and I've to go for some flowers!

SPONGE, JR.—(*bashfully.*)

I'll save you the trouble, and go for them, if you'll allow me.

KATE, (*indifferently.*)

Thanks. [*Gives him the basket.*] And now, Mrs. Busby, let's go. [KATE *crosses to* R. II. SPONGE *follows; offers his arm; she looks at him disdainfully, and exits* R. 1 E. *He turns and looks at* Mrs. B.]

MRS. BUSBY, (*crosses to* R. 1 E.)

I told you you'd get your answer.   [*Exit* R. 1 E.

SPONGE, JR.

I've got it! "Thanks" is brief, but it's expressive! Blessed basket! If roses were rubies and lilies were pearls, I'd fill you till you overflowed! [*Kisses the handle. Exit* R. 1 E.]

SCENE III. — PAUL'S *home; neat room, boxed; door* C. ; *windows* R. L. F. ; *fireplace* R. 2 E. ; *door* R. 3 E.; *door or window* L. II. *Large square of plain carpet laid* C. *Small round table,* C. *spread for two. Arm-chair left of table; book-case up* R. II., *with books seen through glass door. Neat tables at windows,* R. *and* L. F., *with plants on them. Lounge* L. II. *Plain clock and ornaments on mantel; engravings on wall; chintz curtains to windows; fire burning; mat before fireplace; fender, etc. Small vases on mantel, with flowers. Boiling water in tea-kettle. Mat before door.* Mrs. WEIR *discovered busying herself about arrangements of table.*

Enter PAUL, C.   Mrs. WEIR *meets him ; they advance* C.

PAUL.

Well, mother dear, how has the day gone with you?
Pleasantly, I hope. It's been lovely out of doors, and
such days make us all happier, and, I think, better,
mother.

MRS. WEIR.

Where have you been, Paul? You're later than usual.

PAUL.

I've had quite a walk across the park, and amused
myself by starting a pheasant or two, as I came along;
and now I'm quite ready for a cup of tea with you. [Mrs.
WEIR *takes tea-kettle from hob ; pours water in tea-pot to
make tea.*]

MRS. WEIR.

I am delighted to hear you say you feel like enjoying
something, Paul, for I've been dreadfully worried about
you lately.

PAUL.

I am sorry for that, mother.   What has disturbed you?

MRS. WEIR.

Oh! you've looked so pale and wearied on your return
from your duties, and you've slept so little, and been so
restless even in your sleep, that I have been fearful that
things didn't go right at the Towers.

PAUL.

Don't worry for me, mother. Everything is right at
the Towers, so far as I know. I feel my responsibilities
too much, perhaps, for Miss Huntingdon leaves everything
to my judgment; and sometimes I feel ashamed to decide
for her as I have to do. I fear some day she will think
me assuming, and I would rather die than have her
think that of my father's son.

MRS. WEIR.

Never fear that, Paul ; you are too sensitive by half.
But the tea is ready, so sit down, [*they sit,*] and I'll bring
it to you. [*Gives him his tea, etc.*]   Any news at the

Towers, dear ?   Are those men from London there still ?
And Captain Morris, is he there ?

PAUL.

Yes, mother, they are there.   The elder Sponge is the
most provokingly inquisitive and meddlesome of men.
I am as cautious as I know how to be ; but I really
believe that old sinner has possessed himself of every
material fact and circumstance connected with Miss
Huntingdon's affairs.   I never go out of the library, but
I find him prying round my desk when I come back.

MRS. WEIR.

Is the son anything like the father ?

PAUL.

The son is a purse-proud little prig, yet there is something
human in him.   But mother, Captain Morris fills me with
horror.   I curse the reversion every time I see him.   You
should see how insolent he is, ordering about the servants
and everybody; why, he even went to the stables yesterday,
and commanded the stud groom to change Titan's box
and food, and hinted broadly that his word was to be law
in house and stable hereafter, and those who would not
obey him had better go about their business.   Think of
that, mother !

MRS. WEIR.

What does Miss Huntingdon say to all this ?

PAUL.

In the house she is silent.   But the stud groom told me
she looked in at the stables this afternoon, and when she
saw Titan out of his box, she asked him who ordered that ?
He replied "the captain."   "Put Titan back, if you
please," said she, "and take your orders from Mr. Weir
or myself."   That's the only self assertion I've known
her to be guilty of, since he came.

MRS. WEIR.

Do you think she likes him ?

PAUL.

God forbid I should try to judge her heart.   He is constantly with her, hangs over her at her embroidery, and follows her in her walks and visits. Once he tried riding with her, but Jim says she leaped the park palings and ran away from him ; but I don't know ——

MRS. WEIR.

But all this does not concern you, Paul, dear. Why should it disturb you ?

PAUL.

I know I have no right, mother, to desire anything but her happiness and honorable marriage, yet the fear that this man, who, by all repute, is a bankrupt scoundrel, should become her husband, makes me wretched. I have been thinking to-day that her marriage to him was nearer than I supposed. She took her father's will the other day, and read and re-read it ; then asked me for a statement of her accumulated funds, and told me to send for Mr. Oldcastle, her solicitor, some day next week. What do you suppose that means, mother ?

MRS. WEIR.

I don't know what that means, but I don't think she acted like a woman about to marry when she was here to-day. She ——

PAUL.

Was she here to-day, mother ? God bless her for thinking of us—I mean you, mother. Where did she sit ? What did she say ? Tell me all about it from beginning to end. When she ——

MRS. WEIR.

Who ever heard a boy rattle on so ? I can't answer half your questions, my child. She was here this afternoon, and stayed an hour. And so affectionate and gentle ! I could have fancied her my own lost baby daughter grown to womanhood. Do you know, Paul, she looked mostly at your books and your music, and I ——

PAUL.

Did she, mother ? did she ?

MRS. WEIR.

And now I remember, she said herself you did not look

well, and asked me if I thought you overworked, and said,
" Be careful of Paul, Mrs. Weir, for neither of us can
spare him now." I looked at her, and she was smiling
quietly to herself, with just the loveliest color in her
cheeks and such a far-off look in her eyes, I wondered
what she could be thinking of; and she sat so a long time,
and then rose and kissed me, Paul, and went away without another word. [*During this speech* PAUL *has covered
his face with his hands, and at last bows it upon his arms,
so as to hide it completely.*] But what's the matter, dear?
Hold your head up and look at me! What—tears?
[Mrs. WEIR *crosses front to* L. *of* PAUL, *puts her arms
around him, and kisses him on the forehead.*] My darling
boy, what is the matter?

PAUL.

I feel as if I should die, mother—as if I wished to die.

MRS. WEIR.

You have done nothing wrong, Paul, I am certain—yet
what but dishonor could rob life of its sweetness to one
like you?

PAUL.

My honor is unstained, mother; but life is a burthen to
me.

MRS. WEIR.

Why should it be? Trust your mother, my dear boy!
She at least will love you, sympathise with you and cling
to you with the same tenderness with which she first saw
your baby face at peace upon her bosom. Tell me all,
Paul! [*Presses his head to her breast, and kisses him.*]

PAUL.

Mother, I have nothing to tell but what your woman's
heart must know already.

MRS. WEIR.

You have not been mad enough to love her, Paul?

PAUL, (*springing to his feet.*)

If that be madness, I have been mad for years—
ever since I first went to the Towers as manager of the

estates, when she used to come to me as a child to help
her in her tasks. Daily observing her infinite loveliness,
how could I help it? I knew all the time how it would
end—in sorrow and despair. [L. H.]

MRS. WEIR.

Paul! Paul! How could you do it?

PAUL.

Do not reproach me. I knew no good could come to
me from it this side the grave, as well as you do, mother;
but, for all that, I could not help it, and now I have my
punishment—the pain of daily death, without its peace.

MRS. WEIR.

Do you think she suspects your unhappy passion?

PAUL.

She cannot; difficult as restraint has been, I have never
betrayed myself.

MRS. WEIR.

Oh! Paul, you know not how keen a woman's eyes are
to see through the disguises of the heart. The signs of
love, like those of its absence, are discerned by her in the
very air that others breathe unconsciously, as the skilled
woodsman foretells the storm, or presages peace, from the
sighing of the winds and the voiceless speech of Nature.
I hope she does not know it, and will not; for the discovery would exile us from this beloved spot, where we have
lived so many happy years, and where your dear father
lies awaiting me. Tell me—[Mrs. WEIR *falls into chair*
L. *of table, and weeps. Pause.*] — tell me you will over-
come this most unhappy delusion. Do not permit your
life to be withered, and your mother's peace to be
destroyed in your destruction. You have so much besides
her to live for. I am so proud of you, Paul; so hopeful
of you! I am certain you will yet find some woman as
worthy and beautiful as she, to love you and grace your
home, fill it with happy little voices, and hold you to her
by all the ties of a noble wedlock.

PAUL.

Silence ! Oh, silence, mother ! My heart will break. [*Music, plaintive.* PAUL *goes to his mother, falls on his knees and buries his head in her lap ; she bends over him caressingly.*]

CURTAIN.

ACT THIRD.

SCENE I. — *Dancing pavilion. Curtain rises to Lancers' music. Discover company commencing the dance. Floor covered for dancing. Three arches boxed on the sides with arches. Garlands, lanterns, birds, festooned all over scene, and from borders. Statuary and pedestals. Balcony at back, with steps. Small téte-a-téte sofa* L. H. *Calcium on balcony.*

In front set are KATE—SPONGE, Jr., *Earl* DE LA LANDE—*Lady* EMILY, *Countess*—BARCLAY, MORRIS—BERTHA. *Other sets ad libitum. They dance last figure of Lancers, and finish with waltz. As soon as waltz is over, commence horn solo outside. All form in picturesque groups, listening. When* EMILY *commences to speak, they commence to promenade.*

LADY EMILY, (*after a long pause.*)
What delicious music! hear it?

BARCLAY.
Eh? Beg pardon!

EMILY.
The music — don't you hear it?

BARCLAY.
Oh! that's the band from London, playing by the lake.

EARL.
Miss Bertha, if you do not object, we will adjourn to the moonlight and the music. Will you come?

KATE.
Of course she will. Her cavalier looks romantic
F

enough for any amount of moonshine. Quite the bandit,
I declare !

BERTHA.

Certainly. Come, Captain, your arm.

MORRIS, (*aside.*)

I shall have no better opportunity than the present, and
there's no time to lose. I'll play my last card ! Wait a
moment, cousin.

[SPONGE, Jr., *offers his arm to* KATE, *who stands* R. H. Earl
quietly interposes and takes her off. KATE *laughs.*
SPONGE *appears crestfallen, and goes off dejectedly.*
Ladies and gentlemen promenade at back at intervals.
Business to be arranged so that the balcony in back of
the stage will be filled without interfering with the front
of the scene. All must be kept very quiet.]

MORRIS, L.

This is a lovely scene, and should inspire the happiest
emotions. Yet I am wretched — and you are the cause.

BERTHA, C.

I, Gerard ? I have done all in my power to make you
at home, since you arrived. You have been quite master
of the house. Indeed, when you take your departure, I
shall feel almost an intruder when I venture to command
my own servants.

MORRIS.

My presumption has not been without an object. You
know the wishes of your father, as expressed in his will,
and ——

BERTHA.

You need not rehearse them, sir. That he desired I
should marry you for your mother's sake, whom he fondly
loved, is true. But that wish was coupled with another :
that I should be myself the sole judge of your capacity to
make me happy ; that I should exercise prudence in
my choice, if I were called on to make it ; and I shall
faithfully try to do so.

MORRIS.

And do you mean to say that very prudent judgment of yours is against me ?

BERTHA.

I do not say so—*now.* Do not press me for a decision. This is no time for it. Speak of something else, or I shall be forced to leave you.

MORRIS.

It was your father's chief pleasure to give your hand to me, and call us son and daughter. And though his over-weening sense of obligation to you made you his sole heir, and gave me only a pitiful annuity, he yet expected — nay, commanded — that I should share his wealth with you. Dare you deny it ?

BERTHA, (*tenderly.*)

Think you, Gerard, I have forgotten one word my darling father ever spoke to me ? I do remember all. I call to mind, besides, what you were then—a noble boy, brave, generous, clear-eyed, truthful ! Even now I thrill to recollect the childish dreams I had of distant happy years, bound close to yours, I knew not how. After my father died you grew to manhood. You went into the world, and I remained, an orphan girl, at home. I am a woman grown, but still in much a child. I know but little of your life, save, save—rumors which have come to me of reckless dissipation, a gamester's ruin and grosser sins which so affright me that I dare not speak, and will not think, of them.

MORRIS.

And you believe them true, of course, and so condemn me !

BERTHA.

Dare I believe them false when I can read the bitter confirmation in your haggard face and weary eyes ? Can I believe in you and lay my trusting hands in yours, or hope to call you husband, when even my untutored sight commands me to beware ? I will beware ! I do not judge you *now :* and do not force me to decide, by impor-tuning me.

MORRIS, (*seizing her hand.*)

You cannot go till you have answered me. You shall trifle with me no longer.

BERTHA, (*with dignity*).

[*Taking away her hand.*] Your violence does not surprise me, sir. You have had free scope here since I have had control of my property. For two years you have invariably insulted my friends, have been unnecessarily harsh to your inferiors and assumed to rule all my household. With the fullest liberty to invite your friends to the Towers, you have only introduced men such as those who are now here as your guests, and of whose claims on you I am too well informed. Are they your friends or your masters? [MORRIS *angrily seizes her wrist.* Young SPONGE *enters at back, observing what is going on in front of stage.*] Ah, you hurt me! Let go my arm, sir, or I will call for help! Do you not see you are attracting attention? [*Crosses* L. H.]

MORRIS.

Who cares for attention? Not I. I tell you now —— [*Stops and glares at* SPONGE, *Jr., who has been for some moments looking in the door, and now enters and goes round as if he had lost something.* BERTHA *retires up a little* L. H., *looks off the archway down* R. H.]

SPONGE, JR.

Where's my 'at? I can't find the blasted thing anywhere, and the governor wants me to look round after the captain and see that he don't give us the slip. And I have got a cold in my 'ed now. Atchee! Atchee! Where's my 'at? Ah! I say, Captain, I've a message for you and something to say to you on my own account besides.

MORRIS.

Let it wait, then.

SPONGE, JR., (*taking him to one side.*)

It won't wait, then. Colonel Delaire is here, and the governor is just going to ask him what provision he proposes to make for those overdue acceptances of his which we hold from you.

MORRIS.

Hush! Perdition! Where is your father?

SPONGE, JR.

In the balcony—with the rest of the aristocracy. He is game to-night. Go and call him "Sir John," and I'm blessed if I don't think he'd give you up your notes and execute a release of all demands! He's talking to one of the dowagers now about "moonlight effects." Ha! Ha! He says they're "gorgeous!" Lucky the moon don't owe him anything. He'd sell her effects on execution and leave lovers in the dark forever.

MORRIS.

Bertha, I leave you for a moment, but shall return, and you must answer me! [BERTHA, *who has seated* (L. C.) *herself while the conversation is going on, merely looks at* MORRIS *with silent disdain. Exit* MORRIS *at balcony* R. C. *in the greatest haste.*]

SPONGE JR., (C., *running to* BERTHA.)

Hope I've caused no inconvenience.

BERTHA, (L. H.)

Not the slightest, Mr. Sponge, believe me.

SPONGE, JR.

I thought as much. How do you like me as an author?

BERTHA.

You an author?

SPONGE, JR.

Yes, I composed that little romance which set the captain on his travels.

BERTHA, (*rising.*)

Why, Mr. Sponge, did you tell him a—story?

SPONGE, JR.

Yes, and it answered as well as the truth, did n't it? Most lies do, for that matter, you know. They help business wonderfully, and, as for society, it couldn't exist without them.

BERTHA.

Mr. Sponge, you shock me !

SPONGE, JR.

I can't help it. It's the fault of my education. I've heard my governor say a thousand times that lies were like iron, without them we'd all go back to the simplicity of barbarism.

BERTHA.

You have been educated in a strange school of morals, Mr. Sponge.

SPONGE, JR.

I never was at a school of morals. I was brought up to *business*. My governor taught me to calculate interest when I was six years old, and I've been at it ever since. [*Going and returning.*] For all that I'm human ; and upon what word and honor I've got, I can't abide to see Morris even trying to win a woman like you. My governor's loans depend on your death or marriage with the captain ; but I'd rather lose the last penny than have them paid by either event. Don't mind us, and—don't you marry the captain ! [*Going and returning.*] If he bothers you any more, just sweetly ask him where he learned to write, and if he don't run at that, enquire how he spells your uncle Delaire's name. [*Aside.*] There now ! Up goes my half of fifteen thousand, but I've freed my mind.

BERTHA.

I know not how to understand your remarkable confidence, but I thank you for it.

SPONGE, JR.

It's expensive, but—you're welcome !

BERTHA.

I shall not need your talisman to guard me against annoyance. I can protect myself; and while I expect to live as long as God pleases, I hope during the life he vouchsafes me to marry when, where and whom I please.

SPONGE, JR.

That's well said. Now, if you really are obliged to me,

you will do me a favor. I suppose I'm too late, but I'd be
so happy if you'd dance with me once.

BERTHA.

Certainly, Mr. Sponge. There are my tablets; take
anything that's left. [*Hands him her card of dances, with
a pencil attached by a handsome ribbon.*]

SPONGE, JR.

Let's see. [*Reads.*] "Lancers, Captain Morris."
"Quadrille, Mr. Barclay." "Schottische, Captain Morris."
"Polka Redowa, Captain Morris." Hum! There's
nothing mean about him, is there? "Quadrille, Earl
Lande." "Lancers, Captain Morris!!" Let me take this
card among the gentlemen, and we will organize an
American Lynching party and rid the ball of him if you'll
divide the dances fairly between us. He's a perfect
glutton, here as everywhere, by Jove!

BERTHA.

Never mind him, Mr. Sponge. Take any one you fancy.

SPONGE, JR.

I'll take this Lancers from him, and if he don't like it,
I'll dance a polka with him, myself, and make it lively for
him, too!

BERTHA.

Give me my tablets. [*Takes and puts them in her
belt.*] And now —— [SPONGE *thinks* BERTHA *wants him
to promenade with her. He is about to offer his arm
when enter* PAUL WEIR, *who, seeing* Miss HUNTINGDON,
attempts to retire.] Oh! Mr. Weir, come here; give
me your arm to the balcony. Mr. Sponge, it may
comfort you to know that your investment was never
less secure than at present. [SPONGE *goes up stage, stops,
walks back, says* "Ah!" *Meets a little girl, offers his arm to
her and takes her off.*]

PAUL, (*offering his arm to* BERTHA.)

I comply with your wish, but pray do not require me
to ——

[*Voice in the balcony, sings.*]

[BERTHA *and* PAUL *form picture during song.* BERTHA *picks her bouquet to pieces.* PAUL *takes a bud and fastens it to his coat.*]

> Sweet ! good night, I now must leave thee,
> But I know not how to part :
> Every tender thought, believe me,
> Is of thee with all my heart !

[Captain MORRIS *enters on balcony, stands in strong moonlight, and watches* BERTHA *and* PAUL.]

> May thy slumbers be refreshing
> And thy dreams be ever bright.
> Hence, and with thee take my blessing,
> This fond kiss, and then good night !
>
> Yet, Oh ! yet, a moment longer !
> I have something more to say :
> Love at parting seems the stronger,
> But I would not bid thee stay.
>
> Sweet ! I know not why I press thee
> Longer with me to remain,
> Else it be once more to bless thee,
> And to say " Good night," again.

[*At end of song,* MORRIS *advances* C., *and with left arm rudely pushes* PAUL *back* L. H. PAUL *seizes him by the collar with his* R. *hand, and throws* MORRIS *to* L., *and is about to strike him with his* L. *hand when* BERTHA *seizes it. Picture.*]

BERTHA.

For my sake, Paul ; Mr. Weir, forbear. [PAUL *bows low, retires and exit* R. 3 E. Captain MORRIS *follows* PAUL, *crosses and looks after him, and then moves to* R. C.]

MORRIS.

Have you no better occupation than flirting with a low-bred fellow like that—a servant, or little better ? It is disgraceful !

BERTHA, (L. C.)

Captain Morris, how dare you address such language to me ? Mr. Weir is a gentleman and worthy to be the escort of any lady in the land. I have endured too much already. To-morrow, sir, you will leave my house. [*Takes stage* L. H.]

MORRIS.

I have hit the target at last, have I ?   Yes—I will go ;
and leave you to the delicate attentions of this pensioner
on your bounty, and him to your smiles and,—I know not
what besides.

BERTHA, (*going close to him.*)

If I were armed, I think I would kill you.   As it is, I
am without a weapon and only a woman, so I bid you,—go !
[*Pointing to the door, out of which* MORRIS *goes without a
word.* BERTHA *throws herself into a chair,* L. H., *and weeps.*]

Enter KATE, R. C., *meets* MORRIS *going, stops him, looks at
him with disguised contempt, and then comes down stage
to* BERTHA.

KATE.

Why, Bertha, darling, what's the matter ?

BERTHA.

I am ashamed of myself for crying, Kate ; but really I
cannot help it.   Gerard has insulted me so cruelly.   [*Cries.*]
Once that wicked little Sponge got him away by the
queerest story about your father and some dishonored
notes, and afterwards told me the whole tale was a fiction
of his own to relieve me !

KATE.

But how did he impose on the Captain ?   There must
have been some truth to carry *him* off his balance.   I'll
ask papa if ever he endorsed or accepted for Gerard.   I
don't think he did, for he detests him, and won't come
here while Gerard remains your guest.

BERTHA.

That won't be long, for he goes to-morrow.   I told him
to——

KATE.

Oh, you darling, did you ?   [*Kisses her rapturously.*]   I
don't think Mr. Weir will regret him.

BERTHA.

I told him to go because he spoke of Mr. Weir and
myself so outrageously.   Kate, I could have killed him ;
G

and I am sure Mr. Weir would have knocked him down, but for my entreaty to forbear.

KATE.

I wish you hadn't said a word ; but women never can hold their tongues, con—— bless them !

BERTHA.

I am so sorry for Mr. Weir. I wish I could see him and tell him so.

KATE.

I just saw him pass the door. I'll call him. [*Runs to door and calls.*] Mr. Weir ! Here he comes. I don't care to hear your explanation ; but don't ask him for heliotrope, dear — that's *my* prerogative.

[*Exit* KATE, *and enter* PAUL, R. *arch in boxing.*

PAUL.

I did not know you were here, Miss Huntingdon, or I should not have intruded. I thought Miss Delaire called me.

BERTHA.

I do not wonder you are reluctant to enter my presence. Of late, it has only been the prelude to insult. But pray be seated.

PAUL.

Thank you ; I prefer to stand.

BERTHA.

I wished to tell you, Mr. Weir, that no one regrets the many annoyances to which your position has subjected you as much as I ——

PAUL.

Do not distress yourself by thinking of them ; they will soon end, I trust forever.

BERTHA.

What do you mean ? You surely are not intending——

PAUL.

I have determined to seek employment elsewhere.

BERTHA.

Will you really leave us — I mean your mother, Mr.
Weir? She cannot live without you; and if she could,
you ought not to make her desolate.

PAUL.

I shall take her with me wherever I go.

BERTHA.

Is that right? She has lived in her present home for
many years; your dear father died there. No one knows
better than you, who have so often stood with her beside
his grave, the consolations of her widowhood. She will
not long survive the change. Old scenes, old habits and
affections are the life of Age, and, robbed of them, it soon
must droop and die. Have you thought of this?

PAUL, (C.)

I have thought of all this?

BERTHA.

Is my father's memory nothing to you? I remember
as a child how fond he was of you. You came to the
Towers because he wished it. You have been the guardian of his estate. What will it do without you? Can
you abandon your charge to others, and leave your half-
completed plans to ruin, because these ill-bred people
have been rude to you?

PAUL.

I cannot remain without the loss of self-respect; and,
losing that, I should be valueless. There are many men
to be had who can do more than I have done, but with
no stronger devotion to your interests, believe me. I will
help you to select my successor; but I must go as far from
here as steam or sail can carry me.

BERTHA.

Where will you go?

PAUL.

To the New World, where manhood is the test of sta-
tion, and honest deeds outweigh the pride of long
descent.

BERTHA.

Have I deserved this of you, Mr. Weir? What have I done, that you should treat me so? [*Weeps.*]

PAUL.

You have done much ; but naught for which I censure you. You are no more to blame than the flower for its fragrance and beauty. God made you both, and I alone am responsible for my own misery. You have been all goodness and gentleness. From your earliest childhood, your smile has been my heaven, and I have learned, unwillingly, to love you with all the strength of a man's honest devotion, and with a passion that consumes me. You need not tell me how hopeless it is. I know you could not think of me except with the same charity that takes into its fold all those around you, nor would I ask you to do otherwise. I only tell you of my love so you may know, when I am gone, that I have not been ungrateful, nor a deserter from any obligations I owed you. Good bye ! God bless you !

[PAUL *goes from the room* R. II.; *as he disappears she starts up, extends her arms towards the door.*]

BERTHA.

Paul, Paul ! My heart will break ! [*Falls weeping into her chair.*]

Enter KATE, BARCLAY *and* Lady EMILY ; BARCLAY *and* Lady EMILY *remain up stage.*

KATE, (*coming forward alone.*)

Here's a nice child for a birth-day party. Tears to begin the year with, indeed, and all for a nasty man ! I'd like to see the one that could make me cry. Bertha, dear, come ! Every one is asking for you, and the Earl has proposed such a strange thing to please the children, and they are all coming here to do it. Quick, dear, dry your eyes ! That horrid Gerard has taken himself out of the way, and don't let anybody think you're crying for him.

BERTHA.

You're right, Kate, I'll cry no more. [*Crosses right and*

goes to meet Lady EMILY *and* BARCLAY.]   What, have you
so soon tired of dancing ?   I thought with such music you
would keep your feet flying till midnight.

BARCLAY.

The night is rather warm for dancing, you know, and
most of the people seem to prefer going to the lake to
hear the music and see the moonlight on the water.   So
the children have persuaded the Earl to propose some
old fashioned game or other, and he has promised to do
so.   [*All enter ;* SPONGE, Jr. *with two small children hang-
ing on his arms.*]   But here they all come, and he will
explain, himself.

EARL.

Come, Miss Bertha, Kate, all of you, we have a change
in the programme.   The children who don't dance have
persuaded the children who do to play just one game of
hide-and-seek, and I am elected Ringleader, for in truth,
I'd like a run through these old corridors.   I have not
seen them since your father and I were boys.   We have
recruited all this gallant army, and every one is eager for
the fray.—Are you not ?

ALL.

Yes !   Oh yes !   Begin, begin.

LADY EMILY.

Before you convert Bertha's *soiree dansante* into a child's
party you had better ask her permission.

COUNTESS.

Bertha, what do you say ?

BERTHA.

I shall enjoy it extremely.   In fact, I'm the most childish of the party.   I cry like one, anyhow.

KATE.

Except myself, dear.   But we're losing time.   Hurry,
or the romantic ones will return from the lake, and we
shall be forced to dance again.

EARL.

Come, then, begin.   I give you big children one minute to hide—little ones may have two.   [*Music*, P. P. *Little girl binds handkerchief over* Earl's *eyes.*]

CHILD.

How many horses in your father's stable ?

EARL.

Three—white, black and gray.

CHILD.

Turn round three times and catch whom you may. [*They all scamper, talking in a noisy lively manner. Music till on in next scene.* SPONGE, Jr. *follows* KATE *off* R. 1 E.]

SCENE II.—*Corridor in Huntingdon Towers—same as in Act II, Scene II.* KATE *enters* R. 1 E., *goes hastily to* L. 1 E. *to hide.* SPONGE, Jr. *is immediately behind her.   She turns away annoyed, goes to* R. II., *same business.*

SPONGE, JR.

I don't think that's a good place to hide, myself.

KATE.

Don't plague me so.   I've heard nonsense enough.   Go hide yourself and let me alone.   [*Crosses* L. II.]

SPONGE, JR.

It is not nonsense, and I don't want to hide myself or anything else—from you !   Miss Kate, if you refuse to hear me, I'll do something desperate.

KATE.

What a nuisance you are !   Speak, but *do* condense yourself.

SPONGE, JR.

Well, consider me condensed.   Miss Kate, I came down here with no thought but money, I'm afraid.   You have created around me an atmosphere full of happiness and beauty in which I must live, if at all. I have wakened from a horrid dream of selfishness to learn, through you, that life is more than an opportunity to grasp wealth and increase it. I beg you to teach me a better life.

KATE.

His teacher!

SPONGE, JR.

Be my—my—wife, then. That's what I mean, anyhow. Miss Kate, I would die to please you.

KATE.

You had better live to please yourself. I should expire at the thought of undertaking your reformation. I am no missionary for young heathen, and if I were, your case would be hopeless. And then, I have no heart to give a lover. And then—and then—Oh! there are a *thousand* reasons more—don't bother me!

SPONGE, JR.

There's a somebody else hid in them, I suppose?

KATE.

No, sir! I never yet saw a man fit to be loved; and I can't waste time trying to discover him. It is impossible for me to love *anybody*. [*going.*] Good bye!

SPONGE, JR.

Miss Kate!

KATE.

Well?

SPONGE, JR.

If you never tried, how do you know? I used to think so myself, but Lord! how easy it is when you give your mind to it. Just make the effort.

KATE.

I can't and I won't. There's your answer and—good bye. [*going.*]

SPONGE, JR.

Miss Kate!

KATE.

Well?

SPONGE, JR.

Don't be precipitate. I'll give you thirty days to consider — renewable at sixty more — and then accept me at
as many days' 'sight as you like.

KATE.

I don't want thirty seconds, nor any more sights at you
than I have had already. When I fall in love, it will be
at first sight. No ; ·I am resolved. [*Very decidedly.*]

SPONGE, JR.

So am I.

KATE.

On what, pray ?

SPONGE, JR.

On marrying you ; make up your mind to that.

KATE, (*ironically.*)

I pray you for a moderate respite, my lord, between
your judgment and its execution.

SPONGE, JR.

Respite, certainly ; reprieve, never !

KATE.

How considerate ! I feared you were about to put on
the black cap and pronounce sentence at once. I like
your way of wooing ; I do, indeed.

SPONGE, JR.

Well! I told you you'd like it better the more you
tried it. It grows, Miss Kate, like—well, like—compound
interest.

KATE.

If this be love-making, Heaven send me no more of it.
I have talked till I'm weary, so good-bye now, for good.
I'm losing all the fun, and if you don't care yourself, don't
deprive me of it. Good-bye, I say, sir. [*Going.*]

SPONGE, JR.

Good-bye, then. You needn't fear. I'll not announce
our engagement till you are willing.

KATE, (*returning.*)

Our *what*, sir? Who's engaged to you? Are you deaf and blind too? You heard me say I couldn't and I wouldn't.

SPONGE, JR.

That was some time since. You've had lots of time to change your mind; and, being a woman, you've done it, of course.

KATE.

Yes, change my mind as you would change a sovereign, Mr. Moneybags.

SPONGE, JR.

Change it for ha'pence, and give me one. I'll lay it out at love's usurious interest, and win the whole of it before I've done with you.

KATE.

It will only be a change from bad to worse, like this bright evening turning into storm. [*A peal of thunder.*]

SPONGE, JR.

Oh, thunder!

KATE.

You'll make me strike you. [*A flash of lightning.*]

SPONGE, JR.

Well, hit, but hear me! I'd rather you'd strike me than the lightning.

KATE.

I hate you, sir.

SPONGE, JR.

You think you do, but you don't.

KATE.

I'll tell my father.

SPONGE, JR.

Certainly! it's but right the old gentleman should know. I'll speak to him myself, as soon as I see him, and ask his consent.

KATE.

You speak to him if you dare!

H

SPONGE, JR.

That settles it. I never took a dare in my life. Your fate is sealed.

KATE.

Mr. Sponge, please don't tease me so. I don't really hate you, but I can't love you ; and besides——

SPONGE, JR.

I'll say no more. Give me your hand. [*Takes it.* KATE *offers no resistance.*] If I can not be your lover, I'll be your faithful friend. The world is full of changes, Miss Kate, and when they come to you, be the time ever so remote, you will find me still your servant, contented as a dog to obey and protect you.   .

KATE.

And no more love ?

SPONGE, JR.

No more till you awaken it.

KATE.

Come, then, my canine friend ! I'll call you Fido, and make you a velvet collar. [*going.*] Come along for your velvet collar !

SPONGE, JR. (*follows.*)

I swear it shall be of your velvet arms !

[*Exeunt.*

SCENE III.—*Stage dark. Room in Huntingdon Towers, finished with panelled walls, wainscoting, etc. Old pictures of knights and men-at-arms, etc., on walls. High mantelpiece* R. *center, with deep fire-place, apparently built of brick-work. All to show an ancient, disused apartment. Large window,* C., *showing moving clouds, with lightning effects. Wind — shutters rattling. Flashes of lightning, and low, rumbling thunder, with an occasional crash. Stands of armor*

*about stage. Shields and arms grouped. Music of
" Mistletoe Bough " played on tremolo pipes till BER-
THA hides. Doors at right and left.*

Enter BERTHA ; sits down, out of breath.

BERTHA.

What a race I've had ; and not caught yet ! There are
so many horrid stories of this part of the house, that I have
been afraid to come into it. But dear old Busby has lit it
up so brightly, I thought I'd venture in among you, my
lords. [*Looking at portraits.*] I'd like some of you to show
me those old trap-doors papa told me you built in the
olden time. I don't ask you to tell me the naughty pur-
poses you used them for ; oh, no ! you shall keep the
dreadful secrets to yourselves, my dear ancestors ! [*Curt-
seys.*] Hark ! They have actually tracked me here ;
where shall I go ? [*Runs to door,* L. H. 2 E., *unlocks it,
looks out, and returns.*] Ugh ! that place is as dark as a
pocket, and I hate the dark. Sunshine for me, rather than
shadow, any day. I haven't had much of it on this one,
have I ? How fierce and wild the night has grown ! But
it shall pass away before the daylight comes — sweet,
golden hours, that bring me happiness and rest, and him
the knowledge of my hoarded love. My poor Paul ! how
little you know a woman's heart ! To-morrow I will show
you one. Here they come ! [*Noise without.*] I'll squeeze
myself into the recesses of this huge chimney, and perhaps
avoid discovery ; and when they're gone, I'll leave this
shivering atmosphere. [*Gets close into the corner of the
chimney ; the back suddenly turns and shuts her in, and she
disappears with a scream (pause). More noise, and enter
all the party of players, in high glee, and pursuing BERTHA.
All search around in different places, laughing and talking.*

EARL.

We have hunted down our fox, at last.

LADY EMILY.

Where is she ?

. KATE.

I certainly saw her come into this room.

SPONGE, JR., (*drily.*)

You must be mistaken.

KATE, (*angrily.*)

I am not ; I saw her, sir.

SPONGE, JR.

Mistaken, I say ; if you saw her, where is she ?

KATE.

Where your manners are—gone ! I tell you I not only saw her, but heard her scream.

COUNTESS.

There is no place where she could hide. Look, all of you ! [*All look round.*]

BARCLAY.

Here's another door ; she must have escaped by this way. [*Opens the door,* L. 2 E. *All gather behind him, and stretch their necks to look over his shoulder.*] It's very dark. Get me a candle, some of you.

KATE.

[*Going to door,* L. 2 E., *speaks off.*] Oh, Bertha ! Bertha ! Please answer us. Please come out to us. [*Pause.*]

LADY EMILY, (*going to door.*)

Oh, dear ! What *is* the good of tormenting people this way ? Bertha, dear, we're all done playing ! Come out and let us get away from this horrid room.

EARL.

Kate, ask Mrs. Busby for a candle.

SPONGE, JR., (*crosses to* L. *door.*)

Excuse me, but what do you want a candle for ?

EARL.

To ascertain what lies beyond here.

SPONGE, JR.

You can see enough without waiting for lights. I don't like to lead your Lordship, but I am not afraid of the dark. While you're waiting the candle, I'll go on. SPONGE, Jr., *goes in the door and disappears.*]

KATE.

I am so frightened ; I know not why.

COUNTESS.

This is what was to be expected from such low-bred, vulgar games.

LADY EMILY.

I think the low breeding consists in carrying a joke to the stupid length of being disagreeable.

KATE.

Emily! You know Bertha would not do so ; that is why I fear for her. [*Enter* Mrs. BUSBY, *with a candle in each hand*, R. II.] Oh! Mrs. Busby, do you know any place here where she could hide if she would ?

MRS. BUSBY, (*crosses* C.)

What's the matter ? Who's she—and what do you mean, Miss Kate, by "hiding ?" [SPONGE, Jr. *enters precipitately. All turn, alarmed, and huddle together.*] Good Lord ! What's that ?

SPONGE, JR.

Don't be frightened. I've only been examining the balance of this lovely spot.

MRS. BUSBY, (*aside.*)

You plucky little rascal ! What have you been doing down that corridor ?

SPONGE, JR.

'Twas so dark, I don't know myself. I've an impression that I bumped my head. [*To* KATE.] Feel it ! [*Holds his head down to* KATE, *who boxes his ears.*]

EARL.

Could you see anything ?

SPONGE, JR.

There are two rooms opening out on one side, and each was silent and desolate. I could see distinctly when the lightning flashed in the windows. It lit the very cobwebs on the walls. No one could have walked over those floors for many years. The corridor extends to what I judge is an outer wall, meeting the angle of that extending opposite the rooms I speak of. I went to the length of it, and—I saw—(*pause a moment*)—

ALL.

Well! Well! (*Very eagerly.*) What did you see?

SPONGE, JR.

There was nobody there.

ALL.

Pshaw!

EARL.

Might there not be some passage which you did not discern, to the open air? [Mrs. Busby *goes up stage, looking around.*]

SPONGE, JR.

None, I am satisfied. I do not think she ever went in there ; certainly not to the end of the passage. No woman would dare it.

KATE.

Why not, pray?

SPONGE, JR., (*shivering.*)

It's the pokiest place *I* ever was in. I don't mind telling you I did not like it! But for Miss Huntingdon, I respect her so much that if it was for her help I'd go to the ——

KATE, (R. H.)

Hush, Mr. Sponge. [*Putting her hand over his mouth, which he kisses loudly.*]

SPONGE, JR., (C.)

I would, I tell you,—or for you either.

MRS. BUSBY, (*coming down* L. C.)

I have been hoping some of you would explain to me what all this means.

KATE, (R H.)

We were playing hide-and-seek, and Bertha ran in here; we followed, and can't find her. [*Crying.*]

MRS. BUSBY, (*greatly agitated.*)

I'm sure she's playing some trick on us. It's only a little fun, I'm sure. [*Goes up to door* L. H. ; *speaks off.*] Miss Bertha! Oh, Miss Bertha! my dear young mistress! *Please* don't do so in this horrid place. Oh! Oh! [*Crying.*]

SPONGE, JR.

What are you crying for? If you love her, do something. Tell *me* what to do. Give me leave and I'll tear the old place to pieces. I will, by Jove!

MRS. BUSBY.

I know it's only a cruel joke, but there are such awful tales of this part of this house and of these iron-clad wretches! [*Pointing to the pictures. All appear nervous.*]

COUNTESS.

Pshaw! I don't believe a word of it. My lord, let us go! I've stayed too long already.

MRS. BUSBY.

My lady, not one of these men died a peaceful death; but by battle and duel and sword. That one, [*pointing to the one over the door leading to corridor at* L.] after a most dreadful crime, died by his own hands, and——

[*Very strong flash of lightning and loud thunder, with Italian crash. Picture falls. All scream and run to* R. H. *and huddle together.* Mrs. B. *falls in* SPONGE'S *arms and sticks candle in his face; he pushes her over to* BARCLAY. KATE *at almost same moment runs into* SPONGE'S *arms, finds out who it is, runs into* R. *corner screaming. Children catch hold of* SPONGE'S *coat tail* R. *and* L.; *one crawls under his legs; some hug round his legs; all screaming.* SPONGE *stands in an attitude with one hand in his breast.   This action must be done simultaneously.   Thunder and lightning kept up till end.   Ring curtain down, when* Mrs. B. *is pushed from* SPONGE, Jr.]

∽∼CURTAIN.∼∽

ACT FOURTH.

SCENE I. — *Same apartment, and furnished as in Act I, Scene I.* SPONGE, Sr., *and* MORRIS *discovered.* SPONGE *prying round the secretary,* R., *which is closed and locked;* MORRIS *extended on lounge,* L., *smoking.*

SPONGE, SR.

If that fellow had his papers in the Bank of England, they could not be more completely shut up than they are. I'd sacrifice as much for business information as any man of my age ought to; but, as nothing short of felony can get what we want, I think I'll wait.

MORRIS.

Wait for what?

SPONGE, SR.

For what happens next. These providences are occurring in such a remarkable way, that I would not be at all surprised to see the ground open beneath us, and you disappearing in blue fire. It is very painful to reflect that yesterday we had a fête — music and dancing; to-day, confusion and distraction and — death.

MORRIS.

I think it is about time this place had a master, and [*rising*] I believe I'll begin here. What do you want from that secretary, Sponge?

SPONGE, SR.

In the first place, I would like to see old Huntingdon's will.

MORRIS.

I can give you the contents of that from memory; I've studied it, Sponge.

I

SPONGE, SR.

I'd rather see for myself. I want to read it on the spot where it will take effect, if it hasn't already ; and, besides, I've a passion for general information. I want to begin at the top and go to the bottom of this confounded piece of furniture. It's haunted me ever since I've been in the house.

MORRIS.

Why don't you open it, then ?

SPONGE, SR.

I've no keys.

MORRIS.

Oh ! if *that's* all, I will send for them. [*Rings bell on table*, L. ; *enter* LEON, R. 1 E.] Leon, where are the keys of this concern ?

LEON.

Mr. Weir has them.

MORRIS.

Where is he ?

LEON.

He and the son of the gentleman together examine the floors and walls of the apartment where my mistress disappear. They do that all the long night, and find, alas ! nothing.

MORRIS.

Go tell Weir to send the keys to me ; and then pack up your things and be off. Don't let me catch you here to-morrow.

LEON.

I will tell him. [*Exit* c.

SPONGE, SR.

I will lay you something handsome to a chaney orange you don't get them. The fellow guards his post like a watch-dog, and will fight while there's life or the hope of it, or I'm no judge of character.

MORRIS.

He will make no contest with me, you may depend on *that.* If he does, I'll turn locksmith, and make a key of my own.

SPONGE, SR.

What sort of a key?

MORRIS.

The sort that's made of axes and crowbars.

[*Enter* LEON, C. MORRIS *holds out his hand.* LEON *stands silent. After a pause,*]

MORRIS.

Give me the keys. What are you waiting for?

LEON.

I have them not.

MORRIS.

Where are they? Did you see Weir?

LEON.

I do not know. I saw Mr. Weir.

MORRIS.

Did you ask him for the keys?

LEON.

I did.

MORRIS.

What did he say?

LEON.

"Tell Captain Morris that Miss Huntingdon entrusted these keys to me; that I shall be compelled to retain them until she orders otherwise, or proper authority decides to whom they belong. I will go myself to the Captain in one moment."

SPONGE, SR., (*to* MORRIS.)

Didn't I tell you so?

MORRIS.

I do not propose to wait for his royal highness. Leon, bring me an axe!   [*Exit* LEON, C.

SPONGE, SR.

You know what you are doing, I presume. If Miss Huntingdon is alive, you are committing a crime, and I wash my hands of it.

MORRIS.

If she is not alive ?

SPONGE, SR.

You are doing as you please with your own. [*Crosses to* L. H.]

[*Enter* LEON, *with axe, and hands it to* MORRIS. *Exit* LEON.]

MORRIS.

I'll take the chances. I have tried a thousand more desperate. [*Goes to secretary, and is about to split the doors, when* SPONGE, Jr., *enters* C., *very dusty and disturbed.*]

SPONGE, JR.

Hallo, Morris, what in the name of the Seven Dials are you doing, man ?

MORRIS.

I'm going to unlock this cabinet.

SPONGE, JR.

You are using a key that will unlock the doors of Newgate for you, then ; and I'm here for a witness ! Go ahead, my tulip ! [*Brings down chair* C., *and sits astride of it.*

SPONGE, SR. (L. H.)

Johnny, come to my room. I want to speak with you privately. [*Going.* SPONGE, Jr. *does not move.*] Do you hear me ? Why don't you come ?

SPONGE, JR.

I would rather remain where I am, Guv'vy ! I'm tired. What with anxiety and never shutting an eye the livelong night, I'm as badly beat out as you were, Morris, after the last Derby.

MORRIS.

How's that, young Shylock ?

SPONGE, JR.

I'm not worth a shilling to anybody.

MORRIS.

And you have not been able to find her, eh ?

SPONGE, JR.

Not yet. This suspense is horrible ; but if there's foul work, I'll never give up till it's exposed, you may depend.

MORRIS.

I suppose that paragon of virtue, Weir, will be your lieutenant of police till he disappears, too. I expected to hear he had melted into air. I would recommend you to keep your eye on *him* and ——

SPONGE, JR.

Before you say more, let me do a little recommending. I recommend you not to make any insinuation against Miss Huntingdon in my presence.

MORRIS.

Oh ! you do, indeed ! Your impressive suggestions quite overwhelm me.

SPONGE, JR.

This is no time for unnecessary words. Your cousin may be dying or dead beneath her own roof, for what I know. You dare to malign her by a word — yes, by a look — and, though I never harmed the least of God's creatures, I'll kill you as I would a hyena, and hang for it afterwards with pleasure. Remember what I say.

[*Exit* SPONGE, Jr., c.

SPONGE, SR.

[*Who has stood near the door, amazed at this ebullition of his son's temper and spirit.*] What the devil is the matter with everybody in this cursed house ? That boy is fit for Bedlam. I'll go to town and wait for what turns up. If I stay here much longer, *I'll* go crazy, and kill old Busby herself.

MORRIS.

If you make way with that venerable catamaran I'll give you absolution ! Don't go, Sponge, till I appease your curiosity. I am going to unlock this infernal piece of furniture, I tell you.

SPONGE, SR.

No, no ! Don't do it for me. I do not desire to see its

contents. Business may go to the devil ; I am going to London. Open it on your own responsibility.

MORRIS.

On my own responsibility be it then! [*Takes stage a little towards* L. H.; *goes towards the book-case and is about to strike, when enter* PAUL.]

PAUL.

[*Stands between* MORRIS *and book-case.*] I regret to be unable to deliver you the keys you sent for, Captain Morris, but I can not permit the cabinet to be opened.

MORRIS.

When I ask permission it will be time to accord or refuse it. I claim the right for myself.

PAUL, (*leaning on desk.*)

Claim whatever rights you please, sir. This cabinet must not be touched.

MORRIS.

You insolent dog! interfere with me at your peril! Stand out of my way ! [*Lifts the axe. Before he has time to strike a blow,* PAUL *siezes the axe and throws it across the stage* L. H. *Old* SPONGE *leaps nimbly on a sofa.* MORRIS *takes hold of* PAUL, *and they struggle to center of stage ;* PAUL *catches* MORRIS *by the throat and bends him backwards over table* L. C.]

SPONGE, SR.

Help! help! fire! murder! police !

Enter Mrs. BUSBY, SPONGE, Jr., LEON *and other servants.*

SPONGE, JR.

Hurrah! First knock down for us. Pick up your man, Governor! Time !   [*Change.*

SCENE II.—*Housekeeper's room. Two chairs carried on.*
Enter Mrs. BUSBY *and* Mrs. WEIR, (R. H. 1 E.)

MRS. BUSBY.

Sit down, Mrs. Weir, and I will finish what I was

saying. It's so kind of you to come. I don't know which way to turn. I sent yesterday for Mr. Oldcastle, the family lawyer, and I hope he'll show some sense and do something.

MRS. WEIR.

I should suppose Captain Morris would——

MRS. BUSBY.

Don't speak his name, Mrs. Weir, unless you wish to see me go into a fit before your very eyes. *He* do anything? He tried to rob the library this morning, and Mr. Weir caught him at it and knocked him over, just as easy! Oh, you should have seen him crawl off, while Paul stood there as grand as the Duke of Wellington, and young Sponge said prize fight words and hurrahed like mad. That boy's not such a fool as he looks. He is a regular singed cat, in my opinion.

MRS. WEIR.

I am glad he is better than you thought, dear! But Paul has not been near me since—since then, and I hoped I should see him here, if he would not come home to me.

MRS. BUSBY.

Home! I should say not, indeed! He has grown ten years older with fatigue and distress. But that other one is made of whalebone. He is as lively as though he had been taking his rest on beds of roses, instead of climbing through holes and into chimneys, like a crazy cat, for two nights and a day. Whatever happens, I'll never forget him. I asked him this very evening to sit down and eat something. "Not much," says he: "Buzzy," says he, (he calls me "Buzzy," dear, just for fun,) I'll eat when she does, and not before;" and off he went like a race-horse—God bless him!

MRS. WEIR.

Do you fear any one has harmed her?

MRS. BUSBY.

There's one within reach who desires nothing so much as her death, and that's as bad as murder. I should think people's heirs would have some decency. Thank Heaven,

I've no money to leave behind me, and no next of kin to wait around my bed, wishing me gone, and ready to fight for plunder like a pack of wolves, and eat me up before the breath is out of my body! If I was Parliament, I would have a law to —— [*Enter* LEON, L. 1 E.

LEON.

Mr. Oldcastle has arrived, and comes here directly, madam.

MRS. BUSBY.

That's right. Don't mind him, Mrs. Weir. He's fussy and pompous ; but there's more bark than bite in him. Show him up.

[*Exit* LEON, *and enter* Mr. OLDCASTLE, L. 1 E.

MR. OLDCASTLE.

How d'ye do, Mrs. Busby? [*Shaking hands.*] Why, Mrs. Weir, is this you? Bless me, I have not seen you for many a day. It seems but yesterday since—— But never mind. How's Miss Bertha and all the rest?

MRS. BUSBY.

Did you not come in answer to a messenger I sent you?

MR. OLDCASTLE.

I've seen no messenger of yours. I received a letter from Miss Bertha, directing me to prepare some papers of such an extraordinary character, I thought I'd bring them down myself.

MRS. BUSBY.

What were they?

MR. OLDCASTLE.

I don't know as that is any of your business, Mrs. Busby. I'll consider of it, while you are ordering me a cup of tea and some bread and butter. Then send Miss Bertha word I'm here, and ready to attend to business.

MRS. BUSBY.

I'll give you what there is ; but I don't believe there's a bit of bread in the house — we're in such a state !

MR. OLDCASTLE.

No bread? Then give me some toast — I'm not particular !

MRS. BUSBY.

Then you don't know what has happened? Poor lamb!

MR. OLDCASTLE.

Who's a lamb? Where are your senses? If you have any news, make yourself happy, like any other woman, by telling it.

MRS. BUSBY.

It's no pleasure to tell it, I'm sure. Miss Bertha has gone. [Mrs. WEIR and Mrs. BUSBY both cry.]

MR. OLDCASTLE.

Gone? Gone where, you f—oolish woman. Speak, can't you?

MRS. BUSBY.

She hid herself in the Tower rooms, night before last, and we have not been able to find her.

MR. OLDCASTLE.

Who has looked for her?

MRS. BUSBY.

Everybody except Captain Morris, who has only looked into the bottom of every brandy bottle he could lay his hands on. Poor Mrs. Weir's son has nearly killed himself with labor and anxiety; and as for young Sponge — well!

MR. OLDCASTLE.

Humph! What have they done?

MRS. WEIR.

Paul has done all he could do, sir. Without power to act, what more could he do than search for her, day and night?

MR. OLDCASTLE.

Do! Tear the old rookery to pieces. I would have done it, and I will do it now. It's no waste. There's plenty of law for it. She is possibly caught in some of the ancient passages or fallen into some well or crypt. She may be there, and may not! I can't tell what a woman will do. I have been a solicitor in Chancery forty years—

J

but women! I never understood them, and never hope to.
Now, look here! She writes me to prepare conveyances
of all she can dispose of by deed, and leave the grantee's
name in blank for her to fill up. If she had been a man,
I'd have asked for a reason for this! But a woman never
had a reason for anything. I come here and she aggravates
the first surprise by a second downright horror. Never
mind the tea. I'm so furious I could drink aqua-fortis.
Show me the way to these searching youngsters! I'll
give them something to do. [*Mrs.* BUSBY *and* Mrs. WEIR
both try to speak.] No more words. I have heard enough
already. You'll talk me to death. Two to one on it—two
to one on it. [*Exit* OLDCASTLE *rapidly, followed by both
women, who hurry to keep up with him. All talking together.*]

SCENE III.—*Exterior of Huntingdon Towers, showing at
rear of stage a half-ruined wall and tower, overgrown
with ivy, which conceals a small door in center. Trees,
etc. Moonlight rests on the wall.* MORRIS *discovered
pacing to and fro.*

MORRIS.

Is it the terror of undetected crime which thus unmans
me? Speechless under insult, beaten like a dog by the
hirelings of this girl, disgraced even in my own esteem, I
only dream of my revenge. In the very presence of this
catastrophe, which promises to bring me to a golden de-
liverance, I tempt myself to self-destruction! When I
would dare to speak, some ghostly presence lays its
skeleton hand upon my lips and murders speech itself.
Has she vanished forever? Do I believe her dead?
Pshaw! It is a woman's silly scheme to watch me from
some secure retreat and justify herself. But no! She
was resolved to baffle me even before she disappeared,
and had no motive for this juggler's trick. [*Pauses as if
thinking.*] Let me be patient—let me maintain my reason
undisturbed till fate shall spring like sunrise from the
night, or come in the garb of the convicted —— [*Enter
workmen, with tools, led by* LEON, (R. 3 E.,) *who attempt
to cross the stage.*] Ah! who's that?

LEON.

Quick ! This way ! this way !

MORRIS.

Where are you going with these men ?

LEON.

Into the west wing, there. Monsieur Weir will open all the wall to find, perhaps, some trace of my dear mistress. But I delay. Allons, Messieurs !

MORRIS.

By whose permission is this waste attempted ? Not by mine ! I will judge of its necessity. Go back. Lay your hands, without my orders, on a solitary stone of this estate and I'll lodge you where thieves belong.

LEON.

Captain, hear me ! Be not so cruel. It is but a ruin and will early fall into the light of day.

MORRIS.

Silence, sir ! Go, all of you ! [*All retire as they came.*] These fools will pull the Towers about my ears while I am sleeping. I will light a cigar and be my own guardian, for this night at least. [*Tremolo " Mistletoe Bough," until* MORRIS *reads tablet.* MORRIS *lights his cigar and seats himself half* R. II., *facing the ruin.*] My old friend, I will kill the man who breaks one ivy twig from your wrinkled front, and not a bird shall build its nest in your broken stones without my leave. I feel inclined to exile those who nestle there to-night. [*A rustling movement is seen in the ivy.*] Ah ! I will expel you, little trespassers of Nature, as I will drive out every human creature now beneath my roofs ! The change shall be radical when it begins ; by Heaven it shall. [*Rustling continues, and from high up on the wall a bird flutters to the ground and lies there.* MORRIS *picks it up.*] Poor trembler ! You shrink from me as she did—do you ? I'll wring your neck ! No— I won't—just yet. What's this ? [*Finds* BERTHA'S *dancing tablet fastened to its wings ; unfastens it ; lets the bird fly away. Goes to the moonlight.*] As I live—it's a dancing tablet. [*Reads.*] " Lancers, Captain Morris;" "Quadrille, Mr. Barclay;" "Schottische, Captain ——." It's *her* card of dances. All names but Death's! He led her to his festival before the rest of us were done with her. Ha! Ha! [*Advances and looks again at the tablet. Reads by light of cigar.*] Here's my name marked out too! Well, my sweet cousin—I'll lose no time in blotting out yours, believe me. Ah! Merciful Heaven! What is this scrawled beneath it? [*Reads with difficulty.*] "Behind the Tower chimney! Hasten, I am dying. Bertha." [*Comes forward with tablet in his hand.*] Ten thousand curses on me! What devil lured me here to tempt me to a murder? [*Pauses in great excitement.*] Why do I stand with trembling, helpless hands? Am I a demon? No! I'll give the alarm and tear the Tower stone from stone. But wait. I'll think,—I'll think,—of that, which, if I do it not, will swell this tiny banner of her delivering hope to a pall through which no sunlight shall ever come to my damned soul. Oh! what is wealth, if innocent blood drips from every guinea? Or what repose, when every winter's wind shall bear her cries for help and every summer's breeze have freight of dying sighs? If I but dared—but no, no, no, I will not murder her. [*Goes up stage and calls.*] Help! [*Enter* SPONGE, SR., L. 1 E.] Help! Leon, Weir, all of you! Help!

SPONGE, SR.

What is the matter with you that you call for help? You have been drinking far too much of late, and now you look as if you'd seen the ghosts of the whole army of martyrs.

MORRIS, (*advancing.*)

Did you ever see your own ghost? I have seen mine, that's all.

SPONGE, SR.

I only see you in the flesh, and, as usual, the worse for liquor. But drunk or sober, I must speak with you.

MORRIS.

Quick, then!

SPONGE, SR.

You have avoided me for days. I believe you
mean mischief, and I'll have no more trifling. To-morrow
morning I must have your banker's draft for every penny
you owe me. You have enough. I have contrived to see
the accounts of the estate.

MORRIS.

I have no money—nor estate. Cease torturing me.
Go, for God's sake go! Leave me to my better self for
just one minute, I entreat you.

SPONGE, SR.

Obey me, sir, or I will place you before every court in
the land as a bankrupt swindler.

MORRIS.

Get out of my way. [*Crosses to* L. II.] I care not.

SPONGE, SR.

I will do more ; I will make a convict of you. I will see
you handcuffed in the dock, listen to your sentence and
point you out to the street mob as you go chained to your
fellows in crime, to penal servitude. Forger! give me
my money or take the consequences.

MORRIS.

You-shall-have-it. [*Lights a match with which he sets
tablet on fire and then crushes it in his hand and throws it
on the ground, half burned.*]

SPONGE, SR.

What devilish incantation is he performing now ? You
look unearthly, upon my soul! [MORRIS *reels from the
stage* L. 1 E., *and* SPONGE, Sr. *follows.*] He is crazed with
brandy. I'll see he lays no violent hands upon himself
until I am satisfied. Ah! intemperance is a fearful vice!
I always put water in my brandy! [*Exit* SPONGE, Sr.

Enter SPONGE, Jr. *and* PAUL, (L. 2 E.)

PAUL.

The workmen should have been here an hour ago.

SPONGE, JR.

They must come soon. Did you observe my governor and Morris, as we came through the garden? Morris looked like a dead man, galvanized for some hideous resurrection. Where *are* those men? My idea is to commence on the outside wall. This angle is the very spot to begin. I'll show you. [*Goes to the wall.*] Paul, here's an entrance beneath the ivy. It must lead to the old rooms where we have lost her. Hark! [*Listening and motioning* PAUL *to keep still.*] I'd swear I heard a moan. [PAUL *pushes* SPONGE *aside and listens.*]

SPONGE, JR.

Did you not hear a sound? [*Both come down stage.*]

PAUL.

If I could hear one murmur I'd tear each separate stone from stone, though my grave lay beneath them! No, no! I heard no sound save the sighing of the night wind through the ivy and the beating of my heart. It is as still as death itself! [*Advancing* R. H.]

SPONGE, JR.

You are too weary and heart-sick to use your faculties. I swear I heard the moaning of a human voice. Let me go there again.

PAUL.

Don't think I can not hear! I'd know the music of her voice though I lay waiting resurrection. [*"Misletoe Bough" tremolo* P. P. *till drop.*]

SPONGE, JR.

[*Sees the half burned tablet with ribbon attached which* MORRIS *has left on the ground.*] Hallo, hallo! Here's treasure-trove—a pretty ribbon. [*Picks it up.*] I'll tie some flowers up with it for Miss Kate. Here's paper, too, half burned! By Jove, that's queer! [*Looks at it.*] What's this? It's Bertha's tablets, Paul! and here the dance I marked on it myself. Look here, look here.

PAUL.

Give it me. [*Takes and reads.*] "Tower chimney"—

"dying"—give me something, anything to burst this door.
Help! help! [PAUL *siezes some gardener's tool and* SPONGE,
Jr. *another; they break down the door and enter. Everybody
on. All enter* R. *and* L., Mrs. BUSBY, Mrs. WEIR, KATE—*all
the gentlemen and ladies.* Mrs. WEIR *crosses to* L. H. PAUL
returns carrying BERTHA, *senseless, and places her on the
ground.* SPONGE, Jr. *throws his arms around* KATE *joyously.*]

PAUL.

Water, water—quick! some of you! [KATE *kneels by
her and feels her heart.*]

KATE.

There is no life. Too late! too late! [PAUL *falls faint-
ing at her feet. Tableau.*]

CURTAIN.

ACT FIFTH.

SCENE I.—*The same room as in Third Scene of Second Act. A fire is burning in the grate.* Mrs. WEIR *and young* SPONGE *discovered. She is arranging breakfast for one person on a little table, with a bunch of flowers in the center.* SPONGE, Jr., *is at grate, pouring hot water from kettle into teapot, and puts it on the hob.*

MRS. WEIR.

I do not know how to express my gratitude, Mr. Sponge, for all your kindness. [*Sits* L. *of table.*]

SPONGE, JR.

Don't try. It's a deal jollier that you can't. I have made a poor fist at nursing ; but I tried my best, anyhow. [*Sits* R. *of table.*]

MRS. WEIR.

Your cheerful, patient ways have comforted me greatly; and even Paul, as he lay raving with delirium, and always passing in imagination through those dreadful days, would yield to you when no one else could calm him. She has not been here during his three weeks' illness ; but she has done much for us, notwithstanding. And well may she be grateful. He almost died for her.

SPONGE, JR.

She told me she was coming here to-day. She has the medicine to suit his complaint, and I hope she will bring it with her. I know what's the matter with him. I had it so bad myself, in another direction, that I understood it from the start. The truth is, a man

K

never knows another man's heart till he learns he has
one of his own.   Once I could not have distinguished
heartache from toothache ; but now I know all the symp-
toms, if I can't cure the pain. Let me help you. [*Pushes
an easy chair to the table. Music of song of Third Act,
played tremolo, until* PAUL *is seated.*]   There !   Now we
are comfortable, and I will bring Paul in to breakfast.
[*Exit* SPONGE, Jr., R. 3 E.

MRS. WEIR.

I wish she would stay away.   But they must meet, and
why not first beneath his mother's roof ?

[*Re-enter* SPONGE, Jr., *supporting* PAUL, *who is very pale,
and totters with weakness. He sits in arm-chair,* R. *of
table.*]

SPONGE, JR.

Come on, old boy ; here's your chair—sit down. There
you are, as grand as my Lord Mayor.   [*Stands off, admir-
ing him.*]   How are you now ?

PAUL.

I am weaker than I thought.

SPONGE, JR.

Well, you are hardly up to fighting weight.   But all
you have to do is to mind your mammy and Dr. Sponge,
and you will soon be fit to shy your castor in the ring
with any of 'em.

PAUL.

I care little for renewed strength ; though, mother,
when I look at you, I hope for health to serve us when
we commence life in the New World.

MRS. WEIR.

I will not seek to change your determination, Paul.   If
we can find your peace, I can live contented anywhere.

SPONGE, JR.

You talk as if you were going to travel like a blessed
pair of wandering minstrels — Paul with a hand-organ,
and you with a tamborine. Don't think I have nursed
and coddled this man to lose him now.   No, Paul, when

you leave here, you go to London. I have great plans for you. It is to be a combination of brains and character with money, and we'll grow old and rich together. Even my governor says a man like you has a fortune in his hands, and I'm going to have my share of it.

PAUL.

I thank you, John ; but I must leave England.

SPONGE, JR.

Pshaw ! Eat, and don't talk nonsense, or I'll put you in bed and keep you there. Bless me ! While we are talking this toast is freezing. I will make some more. [*Takes a fork and bread from the table, and kneels before the grate to toast it. PAUL takes the flowers from the table and smells them. A knock. Mrs. WEIR goes to the door. Ushers in BERTHA and KATE. Mrs. WEIR and KATE stop to speak with each other. BERTHA goes directly to R. H. of PAUL. He tries to rise, but cannot. She takes his hand, bursts into tears, and bends over the back of the easy-chair.*]

SPONGE, JR.

[*Not observing the arrival, but intent on his toast.*] Bully ! It's as brown as a berry, and raving hot. Whew ! I'm melting ! Here, Mrs. Weir ; give me a plate for this cookery. [KATE *motions* Mrs. WEIR *to keep silent. Takes the plate from table, and stands behind* SPONGE.] I wish I had that icy-hearted Kate here. I'd warm her ! Hold your plate, Mrs. Weir. [*Discovers* KATE, *standing, plate in hand.*] Good morning, Miss Kate. Have a bite ?

KATE.

[*Holding plate at arm's length, as if afraid.*] There's your plate, cook ; but please don't carry your torrid threats into execution. [*Puts toast on table, and retires, in pretended fear of* SPONGE, *across the room, at back, who follows her, fork in hand. KATE sits on sofa, L. H. SPONGE plucks a bouquet at back from plants in window. Mrs. WEIR goes to fireplace.*]

BERTHA, (*to* PAUL.)

I will not try to thank you. I owe my life to your fidelity, and feel, if possible, a deeper gratitude when I.

realize the suffering I have caused you. If I can make you a return, do but speak, and I will gladly obey your wishes.

PAUL.

I have nothing to ask, Miss Huntingdon.

BERTHA.

Are all these friends so lavish of their gifts that they leave others nothing to bestow? You must be happy in such wealth.

PAUL.

They have done more than I could hope from others; and—I am—satisfied.

BERTHA.

I am not satisfied. When I revived after my fall into that horrid pit of death within the Tower walls, I knew you would find me, for my father's sake. When no one came, I slept or fainted; and then after what seemed years of darkness, I heard the twitter of a bird that had its nest behind the wall. I reached my lame hands out and caught at it for company. I wrote those few despairing words upon my tablets, and bound them to my little messenger and loosed it. It fluttered quick away, and then I fancied it would find you and bring you to me. You rescued me from solitary, lingering death, and now you will not let me show my thankfulness. Sickness has made you hard-hearted and perverse.

PAUL.

I am too weak to answer you. What can I do to show you I am neither? [SPONGE advances to KATE; gives her a small bouquet.]

BERTHA.

Come with your mother to the Towers for a change of air, and we will nurse you back to health. Won't we, Kate?

KATE.

Oh, yes! Mr. Sponge will be your cook, and I will go into the scullery myself, and wait on him.

SPONGE, JR.

You will? That settles it. I'll bring him up to-morrow.
Say no more. You have carried your point, so leave my
patient to his breakfast or I shall be compelled to roast
again before my time. [*Pointing to the grate.*]

BERTHA.

Good-bye until to-morrow, Mr. Weir! [*To* Mrs. WEIR.]
I have my own surprise prepared for you, and it may be
you will not think me altogether without sense of obligation to your son. [*Kisses* Mrs. WEIR *affectionately, and
then gives her hand to* PAUL, *who holds it listlessly.* KATE *is
putting on her glove, and gives her hand to* SPONGE, *to fasten
it.*]

SPONGE, JR., (*pause.*)

[*Taking* KATE's *hand.*] He must be awful weak! If I
were him and had my wits and but half that temptation,
I'd never treat her hand so shamefully.

KATE.

How would you treat it, pray?

SPONGE, JR.

I'd give it this—and this—and this. [*Kissing her hand
rapturously.*]

KATE.

[*Pulling her hand away, and holding it at arm's length.*]
Give me some water, quick, to wash my hand.

BERTHA.

You think it perfumed, Kate. You know you do. [*To*
PAUL.] You will not kiss my hand? [PAUL *looks at her,
then kisses her hand.*]

PAUL.

You have repaid me. Good-bye, until to-morrow. I
shall have strength to go, Miss Huntingdon. [*Song music,
tremolo, as before, until change.* BERTHA *and* KATE *go to
the door, accompanied by* SPONGE, Jr. SPONGE, Jr., *and*
KATE *go out.* BERTHA *stands in doorway, looking back.*
Mrs. WEIR *goes to* PAUL, *and takes the hand* BERTHA *has
held.* PAUL *takes it away quickly.*]

PAUL.

Not that, mother. Take the other one. [*Giving her the other hand.*] I'll keep this to myself. [*Change.*]

SCENE II.—*Same set as in Act II, Scene II. Enter* SPONGE, SR., R. 1 E.

SPONGE, SR.

I am a battered old sixpence, that's what I am. It is time I was withdrawn from circulation and melted into a precious old spoon. I can't keep my head with this everlasting game of see-saw. Just look at me! I am gulled out of my money, and down I go. The obstacle to payment is providentially removed, and up I go. The obstacle improvidentially comes to life, and down I go. I trot to London and put the law on my captain's track, and up I go. My captain gives me the slip, gets out of reach, and cuts for France; my revenge follows my money, and down I go. My son remains behind and writes me he has value received from the family, and up I go. I hurry back to get the securities, and my young fool shows me another young fool, and tells me he has determined to take her in full of all demands, and down I go. Nothing sustains me in this vale of tears but trust in Providence, and the luck of sixty years. I hope I'll get another riser pretty soon, and if I do, I'll take good care I don't go down again.

Enter LEON, (L. 1 E.)

A letter for you, sir. [*Gives him a letter.*]

SPONGE, SR.

Thank you. [LEON *starts to go.*] Here, sir! come back. [LEON *returns.*] You're a very nice young man, and here's something for you. [*Feels in his pockets, pulls out a purse, puts on his spectacles and examines its contents carefully.*] Hum! nothing less than half a crown. Never mind, young man, I'll owe it to you. I'd rather be your debtor for a thousand pounds, than cheat you out of a brass farden.

LEON.

Thank you, Monsieur. You are so liberal a gentleman! [*Going.*] I would like to see him in the water of the sea, and call to me for help. Sacré! Ros-bif! [*Exit* L. 1 E.

SPONGE, SR.

I was very near committing an extravagance, but checked myself in time. Now, for my letter. [*Turns it over and over, takes off his spectacles, wipes them and replaces them on his nose as he speaks.*] Who's wasting pen and ink on me? It's a delicate hand,—looks like a woman's— h's and p's long as fishing poles. P'raps it's a billet dux for John! No: there's no "Junior." on it. I'll open it for information, anyhow. Happy to oblige ma'am, if there is no pecuniary risk. Smiles can't unlock my cash box, nor tears either. I've had 'em pour eye-water on me by the bucket full, but I was dry as a duck after a shower. Let's see—let's see. [*Opens it and reads*]: "Mr. John Sponge: In view of the peculiar circumstances under which you advanced moneys to my cousin, Captain Gerard Morris, my solicitor, Mr. Oldcastle, is authorized to arrange with you for payment, in London, upon the surrender by you of all securities. Bertha Huntingdon." Here's my riser—up I go. Now to stay up long enough to get off my see-saw without damage. I'll go to London right away and — [*Crosses and meets* Mr. OLDCASTLE *entering* L. 1 E.]—Hallo! Talk of the Devil, and——

MR. OLDCASTLE.

Sir, I don't know your friend, and don't desire to. I have had instructions to pay your claims against that scape-gallows Morris, in London. Name your time and place, sir, and don't detain me here, sir! [*very loftily.*]

SPONGE, SR.

Hoity-toity — I'm as good a man as you, sir.

MR. OLDCASTLE.

You are not. You're no man at all, by Jove.

SPONGE, SR.

I am.

MR. OLDCASTLE.

You're not.

SPONGE, SR.

Don't contradict me, sir.

MR. OLDCASTLE.

I'll do it a hundred times. You're not, you're not, you're not, sir.

[*Enter* SPONGE, Jr., R. 1 E., *who quietly looks on, greatly enjoying the quarrel.*]

SPONGE, SR.

You're a humbug, sir.

MR. OLDCASTLE.

You're a plunderer, sir, of foolish women.

SPONGE, SR.

I've been plundered, sir—plundered, by Jove—and all the glib-tongued lawyers in the kingdom can't cheat me of my rights. I'll name my time and place for settling this business; and, that disposed of, I'll name another time and place for settling you, sir. I'll send my second to you.

MR. OLDCASTLE.

Oh, yes! your second,—of exchange! I'll pay your first; and, if you send the second, I'll kick your messenger down stairs, you hoary-headed vampire.

SPONGE, SR.

This lawyer calls me a vampire! Bloodsucker yourself, sir! You're an assassin of honest men, with your writs and executions. You're a shield between pickpockets and the law. You're a——

SPONGE, JR. (*advancing* C.)

Hush! hush! impetuous youths. Stop talking like a pair of fish-women; and if you must fight, put up your hands and go at it like men. I'll lay aside family prejudice and see fair. Time!

MR. OLDCASTLE.

Pshaw! We're two old fools, and lost our tempers. I mean you no harm, sir.

SPONGE, SR.

Nor I you, sir. There's my hand. [*They shake hands.*]

MR. OLDCASTLE.

Gentlemen, good morning. [*Going.*] An old rhinoceros and his cub!   [*Exit* OLDCASTLE.

SPONGE, SR.

John, while you are here, and I am getting my breath after my bout of words with that old pettifogger, you'd better read this letter. We're in luck again. Ha! ha! [*Rubs his hands. Hands it to* SPONGE, Jr., *who reads it, then carefully folds it into halves.*]

SPONGE, SR.

That's right, Johnny; you're a credit to me. Neat and business-like — eh, Johnny? Endorse it for filing when you get ink. [SPONGE, Jr., *deliberately tears the paper through the middle, hands one half to his father, crumples the other half, and puts it into his own pocket.*] What are you doing, you loon, you?

SPONGE, JR.

We're partners, are we not?

SPONGE, SR.

Of course we are,—but John—[*entreatingly.*]

SPONGE, JR.

I am dividing the assets of the firm, that's all. I've got my share. Take care of yours, Governor, and endorse it when you get ink. Good bye, Governor. Don't let me detain you. [*Going.*]

SPONGE, SR.

[*Very earnestly.*] But John,——

SPONGE, JR.

Certainly, Governor. You're right. It would be disgraceful to take her money. I'll tell Miss Huntingdon we can't accept her proposition to pay the Captain's debts—of course I will. Don't say another word.

SPONGE, SR.

[*Very angrily.*] But John,——

L

SPONGE, JR.

Of course you feel insulted by it, but she meant it kindly, and you'll excuse her when you cool off.

[*Exit* SPONGE, JR. (L. 1 E.), *followed by his father.*

SPONGE, SR.

Down I go, for good and all, by Jove! [*Exit* L 1 E.

SCENE III.—*The same set as in First Scene of Second Act.* BERTHA *and* OLDCASTLE *discovered.*

MR. OLDCASTLE, (L.)

It is a month since I prepared these deeds of gift; and now that you are threatening to give effect to them, I venture, as your former guardian and present legal adviser, to ask the motives which impel you to this inexplicable act?

BERTHA, (R.)

I suppose a woman may do as she will with her own.

MR. OLDCASTLE.

Your legal right can not be disputed. The law is ass enough to presume that discretion comes to women together with lawful age.

BERTHA.

I have known lawyers and old bachelors still more presuming.

MR. OLDCASTLE.

That's as may be, but if all the law's presumptions were as irrational, it ought to be exterminated.

BERTHA.

You have a right to know my motives. But you must promise me to keep my secret. I am really dying to tell it to some one.

MR. OLDCASTLE, (*aside.*)

Humph! I thought so! I know 'em!

BERTHA.

Now for my reasons. First, a most unlawyer-like impulse to do justice as well as talk it : and next, an irresistible temptation to show the world what you declare has never yet been seen, a sensible woman.

MR. OLDCASTLE.

Riddles, riddles, bosh and nonsense! You are doing that which may affect your life-long happiness.

BERTHA.

I know it well, thank Heaven!

MR. OLDCASTLE.

I have no more to say.

BERTHA, (aside.)

Thank Heaven for that, also. [Aloud.] Give me my precious papers.

MR. OLDCASTLE.

[Throws them on the table.] I wash my hands of all responsibility. It is an act of simple lunacy. What do you suppose your father would say to this most serious nonsense!

BERTHA.

That I am about to pay a debt which he owes, equally with me.

MR. OLDCASTLE.

He had no obligations. If he had a fault, it was extravagant justice.

BERTHA.

I am his daughter, and will be just,—as he was. You will remain, won't you, my dear guardian? There, there, sit down. [Pushing him playfully into a chair.] I'll hold the reins and you can hold—your dear old lawyer's tongue, for once.

MR. OLDCASTLE.

Humph!

Enter LEON, (L. 3 E.)

LEON.

The Earl and Countess de la Lande, and Lady Emily Peele, desire to see Miss Huntingdon. [*Moves sofa down* L. H.]

BERTHA.

Show them up, Leon, please. [*To* Mr. OLDCASTLE.] I have summoned them for witnesses against you, sir.

[*Exit* LEON, *and re-enters ushering the* Earl, Countess *and* Lady EMILY, L. 3 E.]

EARL.

Good morning to you, Bertha. Why, Mr. Oldcastle, how d'ye? [*Gives him the tips of his fingers, which Old-castle takes with profound respect.*] I did not know you were in this part of the world.

MR. OLDCASTLE.

[*With extreme deference.*] I hope your lordship's health is good. [*To the* Countess.] Your ladyship is looking remarkably well, and Lady Emily also. [*Both ladies bow with hauteur and seat themselves* L. H.]

COUNTESS.

We are well, thank you, and very desirous to know what this means, as I presume from the fact of your presence, it is a business, and not a social assembly.

MR. OLDCASTLE.

Certainly, my lady; very good, very good indeed; ha! ha!

LADY EMILY.

I hope you will not delay. I can't bear suspense.

BERTHA.

You shall all know in my good time.

Enter LEON, (L. 3 E.)

LEON.

Mrs. Weir and Mr. Paul Weir. [*Enter* PAUL *leaning on his mother's arm;* BERTHA *goes to meet them; kisses* Mrs.

Weir *and shakes hands with* Paul. *They come forward together.*]   Bertha.
~~Wilson~~

Leon, give Mr. Weir that chair. [*Leon pushes arm-chair forward as directed.*]   Thank you ; you may retire. [Paul *bows to all and seats himself.*   Mrs. Weir *sits.*]

~~BERTHA.~~

My dear old friends, this gentleman has rendered faithful service to me. His care has doubled my estate, and he has saved my life. I hope you honor him.

COUNTESS.

We know it all, poor child. [*To* Paul, *condescendingly.*] Sir, we thank you,—certainly—of course—we thank you.

LADY EMILY.

And pray, sir, add my obligations to her ladyship's.

EARL.

[*Crosses to* Paul, R. H., *and shakes him by the hand.*]   I am proud to shake you by the hand and thank you, too. Command me, sir, at any time. [*Crosses back to sofa,* L. H.

MR. OLDCASTLE.

[*Aside.*]   Humph ! There's the cat in the meal-tub ! I'm prepared for anything. [*To* Paul.]   You've done your duty like a man,—and—and——

BERTHA.

And in the presence of our friends I wish to feebly show my thankfulness.

MR. OLDCASTLE.

You surely do not intend to ——

BERTHA.

I intend to have my way, Mr. Oldcastle. [*Goes to the table, writes upon the papers left there by* Mr. Oldcastle, *and turns to* Paul, *who rises.*]   Mr. Weir, my more than friend, I beg you to accept a most unworthy token of my gratitude. [Paul *rises, takes the papers, stares at them, and drops them on the floor.*]

PAUL.

I could not have believed this of you. I am proud to say I served you with fidelity, and did my simple, honest duty. For that you paid me, as you did your grooms and household servants. If I helped save your life, or made your sufferings more brief, all that you have—nay, all the gold that ever glittered to the sun—could not add to my wealth of happiness in remembering it ; and were I rich enough to make your fortune seem, by comparison, but the daily gains of poverty, I would beggar myself to blot out the recollection of this day. [*Takes* Mrs. WEIR *by the hand.*] Mother, let us go. You cannot think it fitting we should remain. These people think they pay us when they give us gold. [*They make a movement to go.*]

LADY EMILY.

How perfectly romantic !

COUNTESS.

He is quite a hero. I wonder where these low people get such lofty sentiments !

EARL.

He is altogether right, and what he says has the ring of true manhood, madam. [*To* PAUL.] Sir, I honor you.

MR. OLDCASTLE, (*advances.*)

Humph ! He is just as weak as she is. Weir, I knew your father. If he had gained an opportunity like this, he would have taken advantage of it. The recompense is large, but not excessive, *in foro conscientiæ !*

MRS. WEIR.

How can you stab a dead man's memory ? He was a man of honor, truth, and education. His heart was all his life as pure as hers [*pointing to* BERTHA], when she lay in his arms for baptism. He would have scorned the bribe you offer Paul. Lean on my arm, my son ; we'll go together from this house. [*They turn to go up the stage.*]

BERTHA, (*interposing.*)

Before you judge me, I implore you to take these documents and read them honestly.

PAUL.

I will not touch them. It is enough for me to know you wish to pay me. Perish such gifts! and may the giver one day learn——

BERTHA.

I know all now. You will not? Then I will read to you, but only so much as my own hand has written. The rest I estimate as you do. " These gifts are made [*reads*] "to my beloved friend, and, if he will, my future husband, Paul Weir." [*All rise and exclaim,* "Her husband!" *Mrs.* WEIR *exclaims,* "My Paul!" PAUL *makes one step towards* BERTHA, *and extends his hands. She motions him to stop. He stands amazed.*] Yes, hear me, all of you! I have long known his love for me, and felt its blessing on my life. I own my love to-day with greater pride, than if his hand could offer me the coronet of a duke. Mother! [*Crosses to Mrs.* WEIR.] Your hand. [*Takes it.*] I claim your love and his protection against the world. The test of gold was not for you, but that these witnesses of mine should see you as I know you are. I *knew* you would reject my deeds! [PAUL *goes to her, takes her hand, and puts his arm round her waist, and exclaims* "BERTHA!" EMILY *and* Countess *sit.*]

Enter KATE *and* SPONGE, Jr. L. 3 E., *arm in arm.*

KATE, (*down* R. H.)

Bertha, dear, what's all this about? I thought Mr. Weir was here, not for a council of state, but for air and nursing.

MR. OLDCASTLE.

Give him time, my dear; give him time. There'll be plenty of heir and nursing, in good time. Ha! ha! [*Countess and Lady* EMILY *look immensely disgusted.*] Excuse me, ladies!

KATE.

Oh, bother! I have been so pestered by this foolish boy, I could not get in earlier.

SPONGE, JR.

It's no fault of mine. She kept me waiting till I was afraid she had an impediment in her speech, it took her so long to say "Yes." But we—well, in short, we have arranged the terms of a matrimonial copartnership, subject to Miss Bertha's approval and guaranty.

BERTHA.

I'll give you all my aid and counsel.

COUNTESS.

Kate, is this true? I'm positively shocked, amazed, disgusted. What are people coming to?

SPONGE, JR.

To a pair of weddings, I hope, my lady. Are they not, Kate?

KATE.

I am sure I can't help it. You plagued me so.

LADY EMILY.

It is not disgusting, mamma. It's very nice, and so contagious too. I think I could endure plaguing, myself, if that's what they call it. I'll be bridesmaid to you, Kate!

EARL.

I did respect you, sir, for scorning to be bribed with money, but never hesitate to take this glorious gift of a true woman——

PAUL.

I know I am not worthy of her love, but if she thinks——

EARL.

Who can be more worthy a noble woman than a true man? Take her, sir. [*Gives* BERTHA's *hand to* PAUL.] The privilege of caste is fading away. Titles may be and often are the glittering tinsel which but ill conceals base metal: but men like you, who possess patience in adversity, courage in danger, and modesty in the hour of victory, are Nature's Solid Silver.

CURTAIN.

.

www.ingramcontent.com/pod-product-compliance
Lightning Source LLC
Chambersburg PA
CBHW022149020726
47496CB00008B/2629